Host City

David Owen Kelly

PUNCHER & WATTMANN

First published in 2024
Published by Puncher and Wattmann
PO Box 279
Waratah NSW 2298
https://www.puncherandwattmann.com
web@puncherandwattmann.com

ISBN   9781-923099-06-7

Edited by Ed Wright
Typesetting by Morgan Arnett
Cover photo by Anthony Sarow.
Cover design by Miranda Douglas Designs
Printed by Lightning Source International

 A catalogue record for this work is available from the National Library of Australia

This project has been assisted by the Australian Government through Creative Australia, its principal arts investment and advisory body.

Host City

For Jason

Beware of saying to them that sometimes different cities follow one another on the same site and under the same name, born and dying without knowing one another, without communication among themselves.
    Invisible Cities – Italo Calvino

"This is not a Love Song."
    PiL

The order is for two of the Gold Bar's signature martinis. Nic chills two martini glasses and then dashes the ice into the sink, leaving the interior surface of the glass beaded with cold tears. He takes down a crystal perfume atomiser from the shelf and gives each glass two squirts of vermouth.

This image of a man in a black tux wielding a perfume atomiser looks *just so*.

"Now for the signature." Nic adjusts the grind on the dispenser and dusts the interior of each glass with flecks of gold leaf.

"I read that gold can cut the lining of the throat and a person can drown in their own blood," I say.

"The Egyptians imbibed gold for thousands of years," says Nic. "It's meant to extend life, not end it."

He pulls a frost covered bottle from the freezer compartment of the small fridge. He wraps the bottle in a napkin and spanks it until it shoots out frozen slugs of gin.

"I didn't think you could freeze alcohol."

"The freezer is jacked with extra gas," he says, squeezing lemon peel over the glittering drinks to release the oil. "Everything has a freezing point."

Using tweezers and a deft hand, Nic lays twists of pure gold across the icy slurries. Near identical, the twin spirals hang suspended in each glass.

Everything *does* have a freezing point. Memories included. Mine are kept hidden behind unscalable frozen walls. It just takes something related – another memory, a song, a scent, a death, to crack them.

For me, the thaw started with a newspaper report of a death in an ambulance as it sped through the streets of Berlin.

Arno Gatt was the leader of a gang of rich, white, alpha males – the 'Gatt Pack' – sons of prime ministers, and industry leaders – who'd bound down the front stairs of the Gold Bar in polo shirts and deck shoes as if down from the rigging of a yacht in Sydney Harbour.

Arno was 46 when his blood grew cold in the back of that Berlin ambulance.

The papers said it was his damaged heart. All the gold he ingested had failed to do its job. Or maybe he ingested too much.

I wish it wasn't his death that breached the frozen walls, but it's fitting given he helped erect them. When I read of his demise, I felt a flare of triumph. Not just triumph over the death of the man, but over the symbol of everything I never was. I'd outlived the wealth model, like the mongrel outlives the thoroughbred.

I know that sounds pathetic, but I've always had a chip on my shoulder.

There is a lot that is shameful in this recount, not least the trampling over graves, or the betrayal of my own kind by starting this record about the worst years of the disease with a dead heterosexual. I'm sorry about that, but it would be fiction if I started any other way.

Deaths from the gay plague, as it was called, were completely different from other deaths. They carried a stigma combined with a terrible exhaustion that rendered us as mute as extras in a jerky silent movie directed by the Grim Reaper.

Other deaths, car accidents and standard cancers, were full colour and phonic sound.

The velvet curtain closed. It opened. It closed. It opened again. The awful film went on and on.

Sydney in those days was a different city. Emptier, darker, and more beautiful. Rents were cheap and getting the dole was easy. The unemployment office was the only place that knew your real name. Everyone else called you by your camp name. Mine was Kit, short for Kitten, because my last name was Kelly and alliteration was everything when it comes to camp names. You never picked your own. They were bestowed.

In the '80s, when you stepped down from an interstate bus, or off the overnight train at Central to begin your new life, you left the gritty realism of the past behind you on the luggage racks. The '80s was about masks and pretending and adopting a different persona that reflected the 'real' you.

I thought I left my chip behind me on those luggage racks, but it was buried too deep in my shoulder. My chip is built primarily out of hate, and envy, and a suspicion that everyone else had it far easier than me. My chip saved my life.

Arno Gatt once sloshed his drink at me and asked why there were so many gays in hospitality.

Why are fags so servile? is what he really meant.

"So we can tend to magnificent specimens like you," I said, wiping his gold splatter up with a napkin.

Some of us were servile, but for me hospitality was about fulfilling another need. Renovating. Papering over my original family experience with a better one. It was this desire for something better that pulled me here. In the '80s this city was a magnet, Centrepoint Tower a beacon, and Oxford Street the Golden Mile.

Work, and family for me have always been linked. Family and hospitality have always been linked.

ONE

.1.

"Quickly, quickly! Before the man comes!" our mother says, positioning us over the holes in the busted lino. "You sit there, you sit there, and you sit there."

"Why do I have to sit here?" my sister says.

"We may be poor but there's no reason to show it." Our mother rushes away to apply make-up to her bruises. We all have them but ours can be naturally explained away. Kids have lots of accidents.

I come from a large blended family of little money and lots of violence. Eleven children under one roof. Six of ma's, three of our stepfather's, and two shared.

The man coming is Mr Wylie. Mr Wylie is a local entrepreneur. The work he requires is fiddly and best performed by children's fingers, and here he has a lot of children's fingers at his disposal.

A puffing red-faced man bustles in carrying a large cardboard box. A little dog trots at his heels. "Hello!" he cheerily says over the top of the cardboard lid. He motions to his companion, "This is Scotty."

"Welcome to our humble abode," our mother says, clearing a space on the coffee table. "Sorry about the mess. Can I get you a drink?"

His eyes find the dim kitchen, the overflowing bin, and the flies buzzing about the cat bowl. For the first time I see my home through the eyes of another.

"No thanks," he clears his throat. "I should just get started."

From his pocket he pulls out and holds up a strange metallic object the size of a tennis ball, with a plastic stalk sticking out of it. Its shape reminds me of the empty golden barrel of Centrepoint Tower in the centre of Sydney. I've been watching it being jacked up to the top on the news. At first the structure looked stumpy but then it cleared the surrounding buildings and started to shoot like a slow-motion rocket from the Earth.

"Drink servers are implements bartenders jam into bottle necks to deliver the perfect nip," he says. "They do away with wastage and stealing and are the publican's best friend. Your mother will earn seven cents for every completed unit."

"Nine cents," our mother says.

"The agreed amount is seven. Speak to your husband," he says. "Now, if I may continue?"

"Yes, of course." Our mother is flustered.

"A drink server has 13 parts." Mr Wylie pulls the bagged pieces out of the box. "All of them are numbered and their assembly is relatively straight-forward. Then, when they're completed, you'll polish them and then box them ready to be shipped."

I put up my hand.

He nods.

"Where will they go?"

"To restaurants and bars all over the world." He tastes the words. "London, Paris, New York. You name it and that's where they'll go."

"Will they go to Centrepoint Tower in Sydney? It's going to have two revolving restaurants." I can't imagine anything as impressive as two restaurants revolving high over a city.

"They will if the owners want to save on wastage and stealing," he shoots me a wink.

"Yes," our mother says, bitterly. "Who wouldn't want to protect against stealing?"

Once the lesson is complete Mr Wylie rewards us with dog tricks. "Roll over, Scotty," he says. "Play dead."

At the completion of each trick we clap our hands.

"And now for the pièce de résistance."

We look at one another expecting him to pull out a piece of cake because none of us know what a pièce de résistance is.

"Say your prayers."

Scotty puts his front legs up on Mr Wylie's knees and drops his silky head. We clap and make happy noises as if we'd never witnessed praying before.

*

The truckload of parts is delivered the next day. Every afternoon after school we knuckle down to their assembly. We do this for years and assemble tens of thousands.

My role is to fit the pipette in the very centre of the apparatus, and then the cap to hold it in place. This job is difficult for the younger children and awkward for the older. My fingers are the perfect size. I am proud of this ability, can do five in under a minute and can do so for hours.

At the end of the assembling process we have to polish the finished product and remove the exterior fingerprints. The fingerprints encased inside are unreachable and go out all over the world to be dissolved in the first swish of alcohol poured over ice and swallowed. Mine are in every one. The thought of the rich and famous in London, Paris and New York, swilling down my fingerprints keeps my mind alive. It feels like an omen and I start to collect the names of fancy destinations as other kids do the animal cards from the insides of cereal boxes.

The Ritz, Maxim's, Studio 54, The Waldorf, Club 21, Harry's Bar. The boxes of packaged drink servers grow to the ceiling like skyscrapers. At night the ceiling light glows over this city of boxes like the turret of Centrepoint Tower will when it is finished. The dead flies lying in the bottom of the fitting could be diners staring down at me gazing up from the gutter.

*

My second job is bagging hot pies and chips in the kiosk at my local football ground. I am a desiccated looking 12-year-old but eager faces watch me behind the kiosk counter as if I'm as important as the physically gifted boys on the paddock. Or so I fool myself.

Instead of dollars I'm paid with packets of chips, chocolate milk, and any unsold hot leftovers. I share my haul with Ty, a boy who also hangs around the football ground. Ty lives in a children's home and here at the football ground he is a boy, like me, who exists on the periphery. Even further out because he is Aboriginal.

He begs to work in the kiosk, but the owners never let him.

After the game we sit together down by the drain and stuff our faces.

"Do you know what a 'chip on your shoulder' is?" he says, extracting a salt and vinegar chip from the packet.

I watch it disappear into his mouth. "No."

"It's a hurt that people carry around. They feed off it and it affects everything they do."

"Who'd eat that?" I say.

"They're delicious," he says, brushing the crumbs from his chest. "That's the problem with chips. My social worker reckons the worst one to have on your shoulder is a tomato chip because red's the colour of rage."

The rumour is Ty was dumped by his parents in a children's home because he's a poofter.

"I know about the tomato chip shoulder." I think about my stepfather and the time I needed stitches and the time I couldn't walk for three days. "I despise tomato flavour."

.2.

He scans my every move from the head of the dinner table. His meaty hands big as roasts.

His favourite dish is liver. Our mother cooks it with peas and onion. It is always bitter.

Rule number one: eat silently. No talk permitted except from *his* mouth, or from our mother's if it's in response to something *he's* said. Number two: elbows must never make contact with the tabletop. Three: cutlery must be held properly, index fingers cocked and pert. "Proper use of your knives and forks is the only thing that sets you apart from the animals." Four: food must be cut into small neat pieces and loaded securely on the back of the fork. Fork tines must always be on the frown. This is easy because I imagine I'm loading food onto the back of the Sydney Harbour Bridge.

"Concentrate on your food," he barks. He threatens to bash my head and make it ring like a dinner bell.

There are sub-sections to rule four: peas must be crushed and transported on the back of the fork and never in the sympathetic cradle, and every mouthful must contain more than one food type. Loading your fork with just one food suggests you don't like the others, and this is an insult to the host who's worked hard to supply the food.

Five: food must be chewed 16 times before swallowing in a closed noise-less mouth.

Six: eyes must remain downcast on plates and not slide to the television that's left on purely for his enjoyment.

This is torture when something good comes on.

August 1981:

"Welcome to the grand opening of Sydney's Centrepoint Tower," exclaims Ossie Austin, 'Australia's most trusted television reporter', over the noise of an excited crowd. "Where everyone who is anyone is here to celebrate."

I hazard a peek at the screen over the next fork-load.

Stretch limo. Open car door. Besuited man. Woman in fur. Boy, my age, wearing a caramel coloured suit and tie. Camera flash.

Time's up. Drop eyes to plate. Chew. Pretend I don't care about anything other than what's in front of me, and what next to put in my mouth. My ears strain to catch every word.

"Mr Gatt! Mr Gatt!" the interviewer begs. "Gatt Enterprises, your company, built the tower. Your thoughts now it's completed?"

"Centrepoint is our Eiffel Tower," he says, grandly. "And our Statue of Liberty."

"You heard it first here ladies and gentlemen!" Ossie crows. "Sydney is both the Paris, and the New York, of the Southern Hemisphere!"

Slice of liver. Several crushed peas entangled in onion. Push the combination onto the back of the Harbour Bridge with the blade. Lift. Steal a glance.

"Mrs Gatt! You look lovely. Who are you wearing?"

"Isadora, darling," her voice tinkles. "Is there anyone else?"

"And you, young man?" Ossie, tongue-in-cheek, bends to the boy. "Who are you wearing?" The mother whispers something in the boy's ear.

"Zink & Sons," he says proudly, giving a thumbs up. "The best suit-makers in town."

"Spoilt brat," my stepfather growls, looking around.

Drop eyes to plate. Chew food.

"David, I'll wallop you into tomorrow if you glance at that television one more time! Understand? Concentrate on YOUR FOOD."

I nod briskly and prepare to rely purely on my ears.

"With us now is Olaf Ryn, one the architects who designed the tower," Ossie says. "Tell us about this building."

The architect rattles off facts and figures in an accented voice: the tallest building in the Southern Hemisphere, fourth highest in the world. Cyclone and earthquake proof. The golden chamber weighs 2000 tonnes and contains two restaurants and an observation deck. There are 420 windows, a staircase with 1504 steps, and three double deck elevators to transport 2 000 people to the turret every hour, each trip taking 40 seconds. Statistics I know by heart.

"Now that all of the guests have arrived, let's make the ascent," Ossie says. "Catch you after the ad break. Stay tuned!"

I relax and breathe through the ads for Queensland pineapples, P&O Cruises and a new political party called the Health & Hygiene Party.

It's back on.

"Get a load of that!" our stepfather exclaims. "They're using our drink servers!"

I look up. The camera pans through the sky restaurant where our drink servers crown every bottle. A dimple faced, smiling bartender, blond hair flicked open like curtains, concocts a cocktail on cue for the interviewer and the moustachioed architect. A star-shaped stud twinkles in his left ear. It's the first time I've seen our drink servers in action. My fingerprints are inside.

I'm in there. I'm in Centrepoint.

The barman samples his concoction through a short straw. "Sweet as soft drink!" He pretends to fawn for the cameras.

"Look at that poof," my stepfather says.

"He's certainly flamboyant," Ma says, obediently.

My fingerprints are in the barman's mouth. He's tasting me in spirit.

BAM! My head flies through next week, next month, and lands deep into next year. Sour blood taste in my mouth marries with the liver.

"I warned you," my stepfather says.

*

Ma tries to sugar-coat our bruises with pudding. Tapioca, semolina, custard rice, and crème caramels on birthdays, or on completion of a large order of drink servers. It's through sugar she tries to make up for the violence. She folds it in with a begging for forgiveness. A spoonful of sugar is her only answer.

.3.

The first time I set eyes on Sydney is during an Easter road trip in 1983. I am travelling with one stepbrother to visit another who has joined the air force and been transferred to Richmond, at the bottom of the Blue Mountains. My job is to keep the driver awake for the twelve-hour journey.

"There it is," Alan says, pointing his finger over the steering wheel.

I gaze through the windscreen. There's a smallish cluster of buildings in the distance but nothing like I was expecting. It's as if we've gone full circle and found ourselves coming around the backside of Brisbane. "Where's Centrepoint?"

The highway turns to the left and the view shifts. Beyond the hump of the bridge the tower in all its golden glory slides into view like a magic trick.

"Ta da!" I laugh.

I want to go straight to the tower, but Alan turns the car west.

"First thing tomorrow," he says. "Scout's honour."

The next day the three of us catch a silver, double-decker train into town from Penrith.

"Okay," Ross, the eldest says. "I'm the commander on this expedition and you both must do what I say."

"Yes sir!"

"You're the flight lieutenant," he says to Alan, "and second in command."

He turns to me, "You're the cadet."

The train rolls past streets that become shorter and slimmer, and the houses change from occupying their own blocks to being crammed side-by-side like old brown teeth. Train lines converge until there are eight rows. Through the dirty carriage window Centrepoint Tower draws closer and closer.

"The golden turret has eight floors and 420 windows," I explain to my stepbrothers. "It's the highest man-made point in the Southern Hemisphere."

"Give us a break," Ross says.

"Yeah," Alan says. "Put a sock in it."

"A windsock," Ross says.

I'm sure the tower is our destination, but my stepbrothers have other ideas.

"First thing we'll do is go to Kings Cross to see a strip show," the commander says. "We'll see Centrepoint Tower later on."

"You said scout's honour!" I say, turning to the lieutenant.

"Who'd want to see a silly old tower instead of a naked chick?" he says.

I'll betray myself if I say anything more.

We disembark at Kings Cross. The subway smells of piss and train exhaust and cold tiles. It is my first proper subway station and I feel excitement in the pit of my stomach. We ride a long escalator up out of the rubbery, warm, smell of the station and into an entranceway stinking of vomit and wee.

"Hey, fellas," a man yells, from the other side of the road. "Over here! Come over here!"

"What does he want?" I say.

"First rule of the Cross," Ross says, dodging a beggar's outstretched hand. "Ignore the spruikers, and the filthy scabs."

A ratty looking woman grasps my arm, "You boys looking for a good time?"

"No thanks," Ross says.

"What you lookin' at, sweetie?" she slurs.

A real prostitute, I think.

"Give him a break," Ross says. "It's his first time."

"I'm *real* good with first timers," she says.

"Second rule," Ross says, pulling me away. "Always be polite. They've got pimps who can do some damage."

We go to a brothel with a sign out front declaring ownership of 'The World's Biggest Bed'.

We shuffle into a room and sit with a dozen others before a small stage.

When all the plastic chairs are full someone behind the curtain hits a tape recorder's play button and 'S-S-S-Single Bed' comes on. It's a song about a girl telling a bloke who's missed his train that he can stay over. A woman my mother's age with brunette hair, wearing a silky dressing gown and fishnets, slides into the room mouthing the words. On her way to the stage she runs her hand over the shoulders of the men sitting closest.

On stage she swirls her breasts, kicks off her shoes, and peels down her stockings. Her eyes are dull, but I am the only one looking there. The song ends and she drops her remaining garments and stands naked for all eyes to devour her. *Phew. Show over. Now we can go to the tower.*

'Maggie May', a song about an older woman who seduces a schoolboy, comes on. The woman descends the stage stairs and starts moving between the rows of plastic chairs feeling each man's pants as if testing sausages on a grill.

"Oh my," she says loud enough for us all to hear over Rod Stewart's gravel. "Who's a big boy then?"

"Wow," she says to the next. "You've got more than enough."

Her voice draws closer and closer. If I run it'll be a dead giveaway.

I flick frantically through my fantasy boyfriend list. Buck Rogers in the 25th Century, Flash Gordon, Starbuck, Tarzan. None work, and it's too late because the woman is at my row.

She stands over me. I can smell musk perfume and sweat. Her breasts drop in close when she bends.

Her hand finds me completely uncooked. Her eyes express their first sign of interest during the whole show. She finds mine begging, *Please! Don't say a word. Nobody knows!* She signals such a look of tenderness that a lump comes to my throat.

"*You've* got nothing to be ashamed of," she declares, more loudly than she has for any of the others.

After the performance, I follow my stepbrothers down the strip club stairs.

"You've got nothing to be ashamed of," Alan scoffs.

"You really enjoyed that didn't you," Ross says, laughing at the look on my face.

"She's sweet as soft drink!" I pretend to swoon.

Alan shakes his head.

"Hey, that reminds me," Ross says. "You can't come to Kings Cross without seeing the Coca-Cola sign."

Ross leads us across a busy intersection. He brings us to rest against an overpass handrail. Cars and trucks race in and out of the tunnel below. He presents the huge bright red and white sign fixed to the side of a building. "It's better at night when it's all lit up."

It's nothing to write home about.

"It's as big as an Olympic sized swimming pool," Alan says.

"Bigger, I reckon," Ross says.

Alan smirks and points at me, "Big as him?"

"Nothing's that big," Ross laughs and points at Centrepoint Tower standing on the parallel ridgeline. "Not even that!"

"Can we go there now?" I'm sick of being at their mercy. "It's our Eiffel Tower, and our Statue of Liberty."

"Hold ya horses, big boy," Ross warns, scanning the street below as if it's booby-trapped. "William Street is the gutter of the city where all the rubbish washes up."

All I can see are car rental agencies lined up one after the other and a couple of hotels scattered along its dusty length.

"What sort of rubbish?" Alan says.

Ross lowers his voice. "Transvestite prostitutes."

"Fair dinkum?" Alan says.

"Yep," Ross says. "They come right up and ask if ya want a blowjob."

Alan lets out a low whistle. "Well they better not try anything on me!"

"Me neither," I say.

"Some carry knives so watch ya mouths," Ross says. "Just keep walking. Okay?"

"Okay."

We trudge down the footpath. It levels out and exposes us to the traffic departing the city. Faces gaze out from speeding cars.

We haven't walked two blocks before Alan hisses, "There's one!"

An old man wearing stilettos, loose stockings, and a wig stands awkwardly on the corner. I know he's a male because of his knobbly knees and the Adam's apple sticking out of his throat like an arrowhead. He's got a black eye.

"Two o'clock," Ross says.

One much younger. My age. Pretty.

I'm not meant to look but I can't help it. Our eyes lock briefly and from the way the transvestite smirks I can tell he recognises the secret me. We pass two more and I see aspects of myself in each one. The way that one positions his hands. The way that one fingers his own hair. I do all these things. I'm consumed by terror and can't breathe.

Is this where I'm going to end up?

We move past them like soldiers through a Vietnamese village.

We ascend the street to parkland cut in two by the roadway. The tower shoots up on the far side. We're nearly there. We enter a cathedral of trees where the air is cooler and free of traffic grit. Sparkling jets of bright water fan the sky ahead. A band plays somewhere. Tourists mill about taking photos. I can breathe again.

Emerging into sunshine we approach a fountain where a completely naked figure of a man is locked in battle with a bull-headed monster. Shying from the victor, the monster is bigger and stronger than his human counterpart, but his muscular legs are weak and lie almost femininely along the sculpture's stone base.

There are no fountains like this in Brisbane. The only naked carvings of people are high in the pediment of the City Hall where you can't get a good look.

"Hey, that's the minotaur," Alan says.

"He's a goner." The look of resignation on the monster's face says he's known it all along. My eyes shift to the victor's groin and off again like I'm stealing an image from the television set back home. I can't stare too long in case I arouse my step-brothers' suspicions, or myself. My eyes seize on Centrepoint and climb the cables that crisscross to the underside of the golden turret like fishnet stocking.

The stripper said, "You have nothing to be ashamed of."

The minotaur begs to differ.

The lift takes 40 seconds to rocket us to the golden cage.

Sucked in and spat out, I float exhausted to the turret's side to gaze out one of the 420 windows. Cars, the size of fleas, cross beneath the dark grey grill of the Harbour Bridge. The larger mouth of the Opera House is whispering my dirty secret northwards to my mother. My eyes follow the highway home. I wish I'd never come. I wish I was sitting on the torn lino looking up and counting the dead flies in the light fitting. I wonder what will become of me.

.4.

"Ty's Aboriginal," my sister tells my mother, describing a boy from school.

"I know him," I interrupt. "He hangs out at the football field."

"His parents disowned him when he told them he was a poof, and he was put into a children's home." My sister says. "Did you know that?"

I shrug.

"Ty carries a double burden," my mother says. "You tell him he'll always be welcome at our house."

My mother's words fill me with joy.

That is until Ty tells my sister he reckons I'm gay, and she repeats it.

"Is it true?" Ma's voice is a shard of glass.

I give a miniscule nod.

Her voice shatters. "Your life will be miserable, and you'll always be alone."

She flees past the towering boxes of drink servers. The baby crawls after her wailing like an ambulance.

.5.

"I feel bad for telling your sister," Ty says the next time I see him at the football ground. "If you forgive me, I'll take you to the Terminus."

"What's that?"

"A gay bar."

Desire and fear somersault in my heart.

"When?"

"Tonight."

"I don't have any money."

"Me neither," he says. "We're going to make some."

He leads me along the cement drain that empties the creek snaking through the golf course.

He shucks off his singlet, kicks off his thongs and drops his shorts.

"Strip," he says, standing in his undies.

The creek water turns his body shiny bronze.

He shifts his body in the water with concentrated movements.

"What are you doing?" I say.

"Using my feet to search for golf balls."

Shapes writhe from the depths.

"Eels!" I say.

"Do you want money, or not?" He dunks under and resurfaces holding up a ball as if it were a turtle egg.

Distant crack and a golf ball flies over like a satellite.

I strip and jump in.

Ty comes up with two more. "It's chock-a-block!"

With my toes I find a hard, round, object buried in the mud.

I dive.

Over and over we turn in the water like seals and it's not long before we've got a pile of glistening balls drying on the bank.

Ty spots an animal under the bridge.

"It's too big for a rat," I say. "Is it a possum?"

"It's a quoll." Ty says. "Can't you see it's markings?"

Coin-sized markings on its fur are barely discernible in the gloom.

"Aren't they nocturnal?"

"It's sick," he says. "It probably tried to eat a cane toad."

"Maybe it's got rabies," I say.

Three golf carts, two passengers apiece, come whirring over the green and clatter across the wooden bridge. One of the men sees our haul and calls for the others to stop. I recognise him. It's Mr Wylie. He steps out of the cart and stands on the bank.

"I like your initiative." He doesn't recognise me and I'm relieved. He may have asked why I wasn't at home assembling his drink servers.

"Wanna buy some balls?" Ty calls.

"Depends on the price," Mr Wylie says.

Ty sells back to the golfers for 20 cents each. For better brands he gets 50 cents. We make 10 dollars.

"There's a quoll under the bridge," I say. "We reckon it could be sick."

He slides down the bank for a better look.

"Leave it alone. It'll be right."

He has to get one of his mates to pull him back up the bank of the creek using a golf club as a handle. It's funny to watch but Ty and I know not to laugh.

When we look back the quoll has dragged itself up under the furthest reaches of the bridge and we can only see it by the shine of its eyes. We couldn't get it out if we wanted to.

.6.

I wear my Crystal Cylinder T-shirt, jeans and tennis sneakers. Ty wears a singlet top and cut-off jeans.

"There's our destination." Ty points across the road as we exit the arcade above Brunswick Street train station. "Are you ready?"

"Ready."

He grabs my arm in preparation for a gap in the traffic. "Beware of Sodom and Gomorrah."

"Who?"

"You'll see." He pulls me over to the opposite footpath. Two old men sit hunched behind a folding table, right beneath the Terminus sign.

One holds out a religious pamphlet. "Sodom and Gomorrah are down those stairs," he intones.

"Nah. That's you two!" Ty stabs his finger at each of them. "You're Sodom and you're Gomorrah!"

Laughing, he leads me to the head of the stair where he turns with a flourish. "This is just a nightclub called the Terminus. Read the sign."

"Old bastards like that visit the children's home," he says halfway down the stairs into the club. "They're just a bunch of molesters."

The nightclub is large, wood-lined, and low-ceilinged. The only customers are a gaggle of squealing boys and girls. It's hard to tell which is which because of their severe make-up and geometric clothes.

"What are they?' I whisper.

"New Romantics," Ty says. "They're alright once you get to know them."

I see my pimples, mouse-brown hair and regular clothes reflected back at me in their eyes. I see myself dismissed. The New Romantics are snobby wankers. Ty engages them in small talk while I slink away to the bar area. A warmth spreads through me as if I've taken a nip. Drink servers stick out of all the bottle necks. My fingerprints precede me. I was here before any of them.

*

Ty is the first boy I've ever danced with. It's to Blondie's 'Rapture'. I don't know what to do with my feet, or where to put my hands.

"Just relax," he says. "We're allowed to dance. Just don't go with anyone who's been to Sydney. That's rule number one."

"Why?"

"There's a disease called GRID."

I remember the stripper touching me and decide to keep quiet about my own trip.

"How do you know if someone's been to Sydney?"

"Ask in a roundabout way." His words are hard to hear over the song. "Keep an eye out for purple lesions."

"Purple lessons?"

"Lesions! Scabby things all over their bodies."

The idea of sex suddenly becomes even more terrifying.

I touch the spots on my jaw.

"Those are zits, you idiot!" He spins away dancing and then spins back.

"Rule number two," he waves and smiles at a Marilyn Monroe impersonator waiting on the sidelines with a microphone, "don't let anybody root you."

I've never even kissed. I shoot an embarrassed smirk at Marilyn.

"I bet she's been rooted. A lot!"

"Never be rude to drag queens," he hisses. "That's the Golden Rule. Especially not Destiny Star. She'll have your guts for garters."

From the look on Destiny Star's face she's planning an entire outfit.

It happens when she's finished miming 'Diamonds are a Girl's Best Friend'.

Once the applause dies, she switches on the microphone and peers into the crowd.

"Where's Aboriginal Abigail?"

"There!" a New Romantic calls and points at our table.

"Who's Aboriginal Abigail?" I say.

"Me!" Ty says, fiercely. "It's my camp name."

"Who's ya new boyfriend, Abi?" Destiny says, mincing up.

"He's not my boyfriend." Ty crosses his arms. "Destiny Star, this is David. David, this is Destiny Star."

Destiny waves her gloved hand at the woman controlling the lights. "Drop the spot on this one, Ronnie. Not that he needs anymore!"

The light illuminates me and the audience laughs.

"My, my," Destiny Star says. "Look what the cat's dragged in."

"Just take it!" Ty whispers. "She'll pick on someone else soon."

"Now what were you saying earlier?"

I act dumb.

"Cat got your tongue?" She plays me like a mouse. "What's ya camp name, luv?"

"I don't have one," I mumble.

"Everyone's got a camp name, luv. You just haven't been baptised yet. Isn't that right, Abi?"

"Right," Ty mumbles.

"What's your last name, luv?"

"Kelly."

"Any relation to that 'manly' Ned Kelly?"

"No."

"I didn't think so," she says, flicking her electric fingers.

"How about Grace Kelly, luv?" she says, when the laughter dies down. "You don't look like a Grace Kelly. Is this one a Grace Kelly, audience?"

"Nooo!"

"Alliteration works best," she says, picking up my drink. "You know what alliteration is, pet?" She cuts me off before I can say no.

"I baptise you," she empties the glass over my head, "Kitty Kelly!"

The crowd roars.

*

I'm confused by how Ty got the name Aboriginal Abigail, and then it dawns on me. His name Ty, or even his last name, meant nothing to Destiny at his baptism. Ty's camp name is built off his race. You can't fight a camp name though. The more you try the more it digs in like a tick. The only alternative is to stop going to the Terminus, but that will never happen. It's our only escape.

As soon as my final school year finishes, I move into the city and get a job packing supermarket shelves. After so long assembling drink servers I am good and quick at repetitive work but this time the money is all mine. I bleach my hair and buy new clothes. I become a New Romantic.

New Romantics smoke colourful Sobranie cigarettes and use lots of French words like *de jour*, *à la* and *faux pas*. We love winklepicker shoes and high collars. Our god is David Bowie in the 'Ashes to Ashes' video.

"Just don't forget where you came from," Ty says.

"That place is *morte!*" I exhale a puff of scented smoke.

*

The general consensus in the Terminus is a cure will be found before Gay Related Immune Deficiency (G.R.I.D.) makes its way up the eastern seaboard to Brisbane. That the disease will stay in Sydney.

.7.

He's like one of the footballers I used to stare at from the kiosk. Six-foot, broad-shouldered, tanned, brown eyes, dimples, dirty blond hair that constantly needs to be swept off his face. I can't believe he's in the same nightclub. Maybe it's an accident. Maybe he doesn't know it's a gay bar. But how can he not with everybody's eyes on him?

"Who's that?"

Ty turns to look. "Gloria."

"Why's he called Gloria?"

"Because Destiny thinks he's fucking glorious," Ty says bitterly. "But stay away."

"Why?"

"He's a hooker."

Gloria catches me staring and we briefly lock eyes. He finishes his drink and I watch him climb the stairs into the night. He's got a limp and I imagine rubbing Deep Heat into it.

*

The biscuit aisle is my domain because I am both quick and gentle with the pricing gun. I can apply the ticket quickly without smashing any of the delicate merchandise inside. I am pricing and stacking Scotch Fingers when a trolley turns down my aisle.

"Hey, weren't you at the Terminus?" he says, draping himself along the handlebar.

It's really him. The hooker.

"Yeah."

"I nearly didn't recognise you," he says. "Where's your New Romantic

33

threads?"

"I'm a bit of a chameleon," I say.

"Isn't that a lizard?"

"Sort of."

"You don't look like a lizard."

"Ummm…" I say. "Thanks."

"So, this is where you work?"

"Yeah," I say. "Biscuits are my *forte*."

"If you say so." He picks up a packet of Monte Carlos and concentrates on the ingredients. "Which is your favourite?"

"Anything chocolate," I say. "You?"

He shifts his eyes to me.

"I like the biscuit-stacker."

Struck dumb, I impulsively reach out and stroke his black-leather jacket with the pricing gun. It leaves a $1.99 sticker.

I have priced him. I realise my *faux pas* and turn red.

"This cheap, huh?" he laughs.

"I'm sorry!"

"Hey," he says, placing his hand on my shoulder. "Don't sweat it."

I feel the warmth of his fingers sink through my shirt and into my flesh and bone.

"How old are you?" he asks. His eyes drop to my lips as if he'll be able to see my answer.

"Seventeen," I say. "You?"

"Eighteen," he says.

Intoxicated, I don't care what he does for a living. For all I know it could just be a rumour or even a lie. He wants me and that's enough. No one has ever wanted me. He doesn't think I'm too girly, or too affected. Even Ty says he doesn't recognise me anymore. *Good. I don't want to be recognised. That kid is long gone.*

Thinking of Ty makes me remember his warnings.

"Have you been to Sydney?"

He laughs.

"How'd you know?" He wrenches his leather jacket open to reveal a picture of Centrepoint Tower emblazoned in glitter paint down the middle of his black tee-shirt. "Got it from the gift shop."

An omen. Surely a good one.

"What time does your shift finish?" he says.

"10."

"Can I pick you up after work?"

"Yes."

"My name's Johnnie," he says. "Some people call me Gloria, as I think you've heard. I prefer Johnnie."

"Mine's David, but I people call me Kit."

"Pleased to meet you. I'll see you out front."

I notice he's still got a limp as he trolleys away.

After my shift he is outside standing by his machine holding two bike helmets.

The sticker is still on his jacket.

"Have you been on one of these before?" he says, handing me a helmet.

"No."

"Just follow my body." He helps me tie the straps beneath my chin. "When you feel me lean, you lean."

"Have you hurt your leg?"

"I've got a club foot."

I think he means he'd hurt himself nightclub dancing.

"I can rub it for you."

"Let's go," he says.

As he accelerates away I hold on to the sides of his leather jacket. It's Tuesday night and the streets of Brisbane are dead. It's like we're the only two people alive. It's exhilarating, and I wonder if this is what love feels like. We speed across the Story Bridge and the wind unpicks the price tag. It flicks off into the dark.

He lives in Woolloongabba. He leaves the bedroom light off because there's moonlight enough.

He tackles me onto his unmade bed. We wrestle. I pretend we're footballers. The physically blessed ones who steal all the eyes. His lips are the softest and his saliva is sweet.

"Slow down," he says. "Relax." He pulls his face back from mine and does this thing with his eyes where they move from my lips to my chin and back again. It's mesmerising and I must remember it.

He pulls off my shirt.

"Nice," he says.

"I've got nothing on you." I pull at his. "Show me."

He raises his muscular arms above his shaggy blond head. I drag Centrepoint Tower up past his belly button past rib runnels, like lines left in sand. Past his nipples. He is glorious like something from ancient Greece, or Rome. I slide the shirt over his head and smell the warm deodorant from his armpits. I do a quick scan for purple lesions as the material covers his eyes. Nothing, and I'm relieved. Pulling the T-shirt free I drop my mouth to his nipple. It tastes salty.

"You're hungry!" he says.

I fumble for the buckle of his jeans and then the metal button just to let him know how hungry.

"Boy, you're out of control," he laughs. "Let me get your pants off."

He grabs the ends of each of my pant legs, pulls them down, and tosses them into the corner.

He drops his own and hops back into bed dragging the sheet up giving me no time to see what he's got between his legs.

"Let me show you my foot."

"That's not what I want to see."

He ignores me.

"This is my good foot," he says, kicking out a muscled brown leg and wriggling his toes in the moonlight.

"Hello, good foot," I say.

"This is my bad foot." He kicks it free it from the sheet.

Hip down to mid-calf is perfect but the remainder, rendered ghostly by the moonlight, is thinner and shorter and the foot curls like a question mark.

If his foot is a question mark, the answer is I don't care.

"It's ugly isn't it?" he says.

I slide down in the bed and lay my head beside it. "Hello, bad foot," I say. "I like you just as much as your brother."

I kiss it and taste the lanolin left from his woollen sock and the salt from his skin.

He drags me back up to the pillows and kisses me hard for the longest time. As if he's grateful.

Then he starts the other stuff. I've had sex before but nothing like this. He teaches as if the crippled thing in him must give guidance to the chipped thing in me. I do everything he directs like I'm chasing a gold star. We collapse exhausted.

He falls back on his side with a grin, his hair flopping in his face. "That was great," he says. The way he moves his hair out of his eyes makes everything seem rehearsed as if I've been taken, step-by-step, down a well-worn path.

He falls asleep and, in the moonlight, I pull back the sheet.

There, lying naked, is the minotaur.

*

"Last night on the news it said that the gay plague gripping our community is a human strain of African swine fever," muses Destiny into her microphone as she struts about the stage.

"First it was God's wrath, and then a Haitian voodoo curse," she says. "Now it's swine fever."

She shields her eyes properly to take in her dwindling audience.

"I can believe THAT looking at all you *cochons*," she says. "That's French for pigs!"

November 1984:

It's reported that three Queensland babies have died of the gay plague

37

after receiving contaminated blood supplies. The papers claim we did it deliberately. A church leader screams on the television that "the man who gave the blood that killed the three babies is as guilty of their manslaughter as if he had run over their pram in a car." The Premier is interviewed and says, "homosexuals indulge in dirty despicable acts that are beneath the level of animals."

Hatred swarms. Talk-back radio screams for us to be rounded up. G.R.I.D. is definitely here.

*

At the end of my shift I slip the box-cutter I use to open biscuit cartoons down the inside of my boot in case I need to protect myself on the street.

My mother is sporting a black eye when I visit. Says she walked into a door. "You should leave Brisbane," she says. "I can't protect you."

When did you protect me?

"If I go," I say. "I won't be able to protect you."

Placing our empty coffee cups in the sink she turns and takes both my hands in hers. "We're both hopeless," she says, sadly. "Neither of us can protect the other."

.8.

The gathering of religious fanatics at the top of the Terminus stairs swells. Their hymns filter down the stairs like poison gas.

Destiny Star is miming Madonna's 'Burning Up' when the police come swarming down waving torches. "This is a raid," a cop screams through a loud hailer. The music stops.

Destiny screeches back in her microphone, "You interrupted my show!"

The cop flares. "Shut your filthy mouth or you'll be the first one in the lock-up, and you don't want me to describe what'll happen to you in there!"

Officers flip the lids on their little notebooks and demand people's details. Panic grows. Livelihoods are at stake. People will lose their jobs if they are caught patronising the Terminus.

Destiny paces the stage flicking the microphone lead like a lioness flicks her tail in a cage. She coughs and wipes her brow.

"I feel sick," she says, fanning herself with her fingerless gloved hand. "Really, really, sick."

She doubles over and coughs down the microphone barrel. The sound hits the back wall and rebounds.

"The diagnosis is not good," she croaks. "Not good at all. It's the absolute worst."

The contagion spreads. Coughs and sneezes are machine-gunned left, right and centre. People convulse over table-tops and fall jerking off chairs. Spittle flies. No one covers their mouths. The cops panic and lose their minds. Bolt back up the way they've come.

The crowd goes berserk.

"Idiots think it's in the air," Destiny says, wiping the sides of her mouth. "Music, maestro, please."

Our victory is short lived. Bashings increase. Goons capture New Romantics and fling them down the Terminus stairs as if into a pit. That's when the murmurs start: a law is being introduced to make it illegal for 'Deviants and Perverts' to congregate.

I'm congregating at the bar with the New Romantics when Johnnie Minotaur comes in. I've been ignoring his calls and hiding in the back of the shop when I see him pushing his trolley through the supermarket.

The New Romantics are talking about abandoning Queensland.

"Homosexuality is legal in NSW," one man says.

"But that's where the disease is running rampant," another replies.

Johnnie slides up to me, "Wanna drink?"

"No."

"What's got up your nose?"

It's not the reason but it's the easiest and kindest one to use. "You never told me you were a hooker."

"You never told me I should have charged." He turns away.

*

"I'm moving to Sydney," I tell Ty.

"Out of the frying pan into the fire."

"At least we're legal there."

"Yeah but for how long?"

"Anything is better than here."

"Everyone's leaving and going south," Destiny peers out into the small crowd. "Hey, that reminds me. What did the nymphomaniac say to the necrophiliac?"

"What?" a New Romantic calls.

"Fuck me dead!"

The New Romantic groans.

*

I book a seat on an Olympic coach for the 12-hour journey south. A gaggle of New Romantics, done up to the nines in all their make-up and trailing streamers and balloons come to bid me *adieu*. 'Make us proud,' they sing. 'Make a fortune.' Someone presses a sleeping pill in my hand as a farewell gift so I can sleep the bulk of the journey. Ty gives me the address of a friend of a friend, a guy called Donna, or Donut, who'd abandoned Brisbane a few months before and rumoured to be living in Bondi. Goodbye Darren, Bruce, Lee Bee, Jane! Au revoir Tim! See ya, Shane!

I play Bronski Beat's 'Smalltown Boy' on my Walkman till the pill takes effect and I nod off. I wake during the night and my eyes chase the frantic yellow square of headlight as it flits, mile after mile, over the pale eucalyptus crowding the highway edge like the ghosts of all the people who ever lived.

Two

.1.

Oxford Street's Golden Mile starts at Hyde Park's Emden Gun, hinges on Gilligan's Island at Taylor Square, and terminates at Victoria Barracks. Entering it is akin to walking into a jungle. Mind your step. Watch your belongings. There are centipedes and snakes, flowers of exquisite beauty, and flesh eaters. There's always been more blood than gold.

*

The days don't seem like days. We wake at 1pm and are lucky if we make it down in time for a swim before we have to start getting ready to go out again on Oxford Street.

Sam's our leader. She's an uncontrollable 16-year-old, given free reign of her father's investment property – a two-bedroom, two-bathroom, top floor Bondi apartment – while he finalises his divorce from her mother. Sam's a poor little rich girl with Daddy issues and we're her living dolls she's filled the apartment with, in retaliation. It's her way or the highway back to Brisbane.

My problem is the apartment is full and Sam keeps repeating that there isn't enough room for another Brisbane refugee. If I'm going to stay, I have to prove my worth.

Cocooned in a warm haze of alcohol and speed we parade onto the 380 bus.

"Oxford Street, please." We pay our fare and swagger up the aisle.

Donut's purple mohawk slices through the air like a shark's fin. The passengers have seen punks before but not one wearing an orange sarong and green platform thongs. From the looks on the passengers' faces they can't tell which of us has a dick and which hasn't.

"We must look like creatures from outer space," Toni, following him, laughs. Toni is Sam's best friend from school and her look is '60s gangster's moll. False eyelashes, pencil skirt, and big blonde bouffant.

"It's a cheap thrill," Lana says, in all his glory. The hours he takes to get ready is worth it because when he's finished, he looks like a Hollywood goddess. Lana Turner is his favourite. Hence his name.

"For us, or them?" Mort, behind him, peers out from beneath his crystalline midnight blue fringe. He's all Goth; crucifixes, stovepipe jeans, deathly pale make-up. Mort's short for Morticia – Destiny Star's play on Morris.

Lana looks back. "Them. What they think has zero effect on me."

Sam's next. She's the most masculine looking of us all. Her snub-nose is pierced and splattered with large freckles that refuse to be disguised by foundation. Her black, dreadlocked hair is tied up in a chunky top knot and she has 10 earrings in each ear. She could be a Persian warrior except for her Mickey Mouse T-shirt.

I'm last. The passengers eye me up and down.

Jesus fucking Christ, look at this one.

I'm not a drag queen, and I don't want to be female. I don't wear wigs or fake breasts. I'm not punk or New Romantic because those phases are old.

I look like a skinhead chick who's swallowed a disco ball. Albino bleached hair, long fringe back and front, crown and sides shaved to a fuzz. Mascara brows. Bandit eyes rimmed in black kohl. Silver dangly earrings. Red and black midriff top, tight tube skirt, fishnets disappearing into my high-heeled boots. I don't tuck. The only tucking I do is the box-cutter I brought with me from Brisbane pushed down the inside of my boot. Let them stare daggers. I've got a real one, honey. Come near me and I'll slice you open like a biscuit box.

"What the fuck are you lot?" one old man asks.

"Hybrid creatures of a new world," Lana purrs. "You get it, or you don't."

We position ourselves by the bus's middle swing-doors. Donut spots a drunk slumped against a window and sits down next to him.

He nods to Sam and Sam nods to Lana as the bus accelerates up Bondi Road.

"Stop scaring the locals," Sam says, meaning she wants the exact opposite.

"You have to be ready anywhere, anytime," Lana slips out his mirrored compact and starts to powder his face. "Just like Miss Turner."

A cloud of sweet-smelling cosmetic dust permeates the air.

The outrage in the passengers' eyes is delicious.

"Freak," is lobbed from a hidden mouth.

Lana continues powdering.

"Call me freak," Lana sings for the entire bus, "then freak is what you'll get."

He slides the compact away and starts swinging about the pole striking poses like a fashion model.

"Woohoo!" Sam catcalls. "Yeah!"

The passengers can't take their eyes off him which is exactly the desired effect. Even the driver's eyes are glued to the rear vision. None of them witness Donut going through the drunk's pockets.

"I'm going to throw you off if you all don't sit down," the driver calls over his shoulder.

Donut hides what he finds and nods to Sam.

"Too late!" Sam pulls the cord. "We're getting off."

.2.

Each nightclub and pub on Oxford Street has its own demographic. The Albury specialises in the All-American. The Oxford is Aussie – flannos and work gear. The Midnight Shift pulls moustachioed leather clones and their colour-coded handkerchiefs. We haunt the Exchange – *Sexchange* – Hotel. If we're not inside dancing or thieving, we're outside sitting on the long front step listening to the music pouring out and giving cheek to the taxi drivers leaning smoking against their car bonnets while running their eyes over us.

*

The money from the drunk's wallet has been spent. Sam nods to Mort. "Let the test begin."

'Dead Eyes Opened' by Severed Heads is blaring as Mort leads me past the bouncers into the front bar called Saddletramps. I see my trusty touch-stones crammed into the bottle necks on the bar shelves. My fingerprints proceed me. I've been here forever.

We jostle past a crowded dancefloor and push through into a quieter bar where a hundred old bathroom cabinet mirrors, dressing table mirrors, cupboard mirrors are arranged up lilac-painted walls.

"This is the Ragtime Follies Bar," Mort says, from beneath his long fringe of midnight blue. "Most people call it the Mirror Bar. We call it God's Waiting Room."

It's not hard to see why.

Husks of men stand whispering among the regular looking patrons like escapees from a concentration camp. Behind them the antique shapes of the mirrors rear up like headstones.

"Why would they want to see themselves in all these mirrors?"

Mort shrugs. "No one knows, but it's is the hardest bar to steal from because of all the reflections."

'Thinking of You', by Sister Sledge comes on and the crowd starts to sway and shuffle.

"These are the rules," Mort says. "One: don't steal drinks from the sick ones. Two: always drink through a fresh straw. If one's been left in a drink, discard it. Three: all spoils are shared. And if you're caught, you're on your own."

"Remind me what the winner gets?"

"A roof over their head," he says. "Your test starts now."

He walks to the other side of the room to monitor my progress.

Some of the sick ones smile weakly in lost reverie, others simply stand looking bewildered. Eyes are everywhere watching everyone. I take my time before choosing a target. Life has trained me for this. I stare down at my plate and debate which corner of liver to cut next.

A man stands alone at a table with a drink sweating on a coaster before him. His head moves to the music and his fingers clip invisible bongo drums. He doesn't look sick.

I casually sidle up. Lost in music, or memories, he doesn't register my presence. Good. I glance about pretending I am waiting for a rendezvous.

The song reaches its crescendo. The man lifts his face to the ceiling, as if to heaven. A single tear slides down his cheek. If I don't do it now I'll be kicked out of the house and have to return to Queensland. I lift his drink and scurry away.

"Bourbon and coke," Mort waves the glass beneath his nose. "Sam's favourite."

Outside we drop our black straws in like elephant trunks.

"The alcohol kills the germs," Sam says. "Never put your lips to the rim. You don't want to get sick."

"Have I passed?"

"There's one more test," she says.

.3.

These are the days of strange rumours. Talk that you can catch the gay plague from kissing, or from a mosquito bite. Talk of the government building a wall around Darlinghurst to keep the plague contained, of aerial bombardments to keep the mozzies down. Talk of old quarantine stations around Australia being reopened, of the army being used to round up all the poofters. Bashings increase tenfold. You're dead meat if you don't have a gang to watch your back.

*

Sam motions me. I follow her over the footpath's constellations of trodden gum and crushed cigarette butts.

"Have you ever scabbed?" she says.

My heart drops remembering the extended hands outside Kings Cross train station the first time I came to Sydney. I thought thieving was bad enough.

"No."

"Ok, these are the rules. Number one: never scab drunk. You've got to stay alert. Two: remember your manners. Say please and thank-you."

I'm nodding like David Bowie to his mother in the 'Ashes to Ashes' video.

"Number three: only ever ask for 20 cents. You'll get less knockbacks. If you get more it's a bonus. This is a numbers game. The more targets you ask, the more you get. Number four: never give a thing away. Not even directions. Make 'em pay. Number five: if you hear this warning whistle, run or hide." Sam inserts two fingers in her mouth and lets fly. "It means a centipede is coming."

"What's a centipede?"

"A skinhead gang running in single file. That's how they move."

My scabbing spot is on the corner of Riley and Oxford Streets opposite the interstate bus terminal. Not too bright, not too dark, and not too far. Not too bright that I stand out like a beacon saying, Here I am. Come get me, and not too dark that no one can see what's happening if they do come, and not too far that I can't run back if Sam whistles her warning.

"Your spot is paved with gold," Sam says as a Pioneer bus disgorges its passengers like a drunk against a wall. "With a wealth of pedestrians."

Drink stealing is done in the dark, but here the people arriving on every bus from Brisbane will see me illuminated in the streetlight with my hand extended. Word that I've been reduced to begging will reach home. He's a beggar? Maybe Ty will hear and feel shame for me. But there's no going back. Hopefully no one will recognise me.

I approach a businessman, "Do you have any change?"

He ignores me and increases his walking speed.

I hear a ship's horn from the harbour bemoaning my failure.

"Be polite," Sam says.

A cab stops against the opposite corner. The interior light illuminates three paying passengers, all with scraped back ponytails. Two blonds and a big redhead. One of the blonds pays while the other hops out and attends to the redhead's door. Red's suit changes from burgundy, to purple, to oil slick as he slides out. The taxi pulls away and the blond pair circle him, smoothing his double-breasted jacket of wrinkles and correcting any stray red hair. Their rolled-up sleeves reveal gold watches thick as shackles gleaming against their wrists.

I move forward to demonstrate to Sam I'm keen to apply all her lessons. She seizes my arm.

"Beware the Pied Piper," she says. "That's the Golden Rule."

"Who?"

"He's a pimp and all his boys are sick. He's out looking for fresh blood. You stay here and practise scabbing while I go warn the others."

.4.

In the lull between the arrival and departure of interstate buses my scabbing corner goes quiet.

A ship's horn echoes up from the harbour, "*Oooooooooo.*" It sounds like the same one from earlier.

"Do you hear her?" a soft voice says.

I turn to see a figure emerging out of the shadows keeping close to the hard flank of the building. He glances up and the streetlight catches his face under his hat brim. His eyes are fever bright and the spots on his face make me think of the sick quoll under the golf course bridge.

"Excuse me?" I say.

"I heard her coming from my balcony." He undulates his hand at an apartment block behind him. The movement causes him to topple. His hat falls.

"Whoa!" I leap forward and catch his sleeve.

He's nothing but skin and bone and purple spots are everywhere.

Purple lessons.

"Don't touch me." He hisses sinking to the footpath like a deflating balloon. I let him deflate.

"The drugs give me vertigo," he whispers.

"*Oooooooooo,*" The horn calls again.

His head perks. "There!"

"That's a ship," I say.

He lets loose an insane laugh, "A spaceship! An Unidentified Flying Object!"

His lolling head reveals gapped front teeth, and a twinkling star stud in his left ear.

Centrepoint Tower. Opening night on the television. The sky restaurant. The bartender flicks his blond hair, smiles a gap-toothed smile, and tastes me in spirit.

"Did you work at Centrepoint?"

"That's none of your damn business," he hisses.

"Fine." I kick him his hat. It lands short and he has to stretch out to reach it. I feel sick that I made him.

I return to my job, but no pedestrian will stop when they see the muttering creature on the ground behind me.

He croaks at me. "Speaking of business, are you a whore?"

"What?"

"Prostituting. Renting. Hooking."

"I'm a scab."

"Good night, is it? For scabbing?" he sounds dubious.

"It was." Another pedestrian scuttles by.

"I'm scaring your customers away," he says, sadly.

"I didn't mean it like that."

"Of course you did," he sighs. "Let's call a spade a spade... or a scab a scab."

"Please don't." I want him to go back where he came from so I can earn my keep.

"Why don't you get a real job?" He scratches himself absently.

"Mind your own damn business."

"Touché."

"I used to work at Centrepoint in the Sky Restaurant." His voice has a wandering quality as if he's not really speaking to me. "It's where I met Olaf, the love of my life. He was one of the architects, but I don't work anywhere anymore. I haven't for ages."

I feel bad. He is sick after all and, from the sounds of it, his boyfriend has died.

"What's the point of working if they're just going to transport us all to a quarantine island?" I say.

"*Oooooooooo.*" The ship's horn sounds much closer as if the freighter is heading directly for us.

"For me, the only transportation will be upwards." He hoists himself to his feet and totters unsteadily to the edge of the footpath. "Here she comes. My queen."

He wraps his arms about the telegraph pole and, leaning his head against the splintered trunk, gazes with adoration up the roadway.

A woman sheathed in palest pink glides regally down the middle of Oxford Street, almost floating. Her arms are encased in long pale opera gloves and her glossy midnight black hair is twined up and clamped by a twinkling tiara.

"She's going to get hit by a car," I say.

"The universe protects her," he corrects. "She's a supernatural being."

You really are delirious, I think.

The woman stops, lifts a gloved hand, and tilts her head. Her throat releases a capsule of burnished, mournful "*Oooooooooo.*"

The orb of sound revolves in the middle of the street before zooming off. She *is* the ship's horn.

"I thought that sound was coming from the harbour."

"She is the harbour, the harbour master, the ship builder, and the ship. She is our only way upwards." He casts his eyes sadly about. "Oxford Street is full of ghosts. Her cry transports us to the big dancehall in the sky."

"Hallelujah," I play along.

"Olaf used to say Oxford Street is a river and she is our spiritual egret," he says in a faraway voice. "With a cry of her voice she releases those of us that have passed from their earthly bounds."

"*Oooooooooo!*" The sound hovers in the street before shooting skywards.

"Established religions despise us," he says, quietly. "We find our own means of heavenly transport. Most of my friends are already there…"

"I'm sorry for your loss."

"Here you go, Scab." He pulls out a handful of coins. "For your lost customers."

"Thank you," I say, as money tinkles like rain into my open palm.

"You failed school, did you?"

"I did okay at art," I said.

"This must make an interesting picture, don't you think?" he says, scratching a lesion on his arm as another pedestrian slips by. "Us two shooting the breeze. You could title it a pair of no-hopers."

"Do they hurt?" I ask.

"What?"

I remember the word, "Your lesions."

"They itch."

I tell him about the time I misheard the word 'lesions' for 'lessons'.

"Was 'lessons' the first thing that sprung to mind when you saw me?"

"No," I say. "I pictured a quoll."

"I like that," he says. "A nocturnal Australian creature covered in spots. I will call you Scab, and you must call me Quoll."

.5.

"Who is the singing woman?" I ask Sam when I meet the gang on the front step of the Exchange to hand over the money.

"The Opera Lady," she says, building silver towers on the step like a child on the beach makes sandcastles. "Now don't interrupt when I'm counting."

"Sorry," I said.

"She's a real opera singer," Toni explains. "She lost her mind when she lost her voice, and she comes out at night to try to find both again."

"It's the street acoustics," Mort says. "She tests the same note over and over searching for its flaw."

"She's the epitome of tragedy," Lana says, reverently.

I prefer Quoll's version but I'm not going to mention him in case they try to ingratiate themselves and feather their own nests.

"You've earned the most tonight," Sam tells me. "You're the winner."

"Hey, that's not fair," Donut whinges. "I stole the wallet."

"With *just* a little bit of help from your friends," Lana retorts.

"All you did was powder your stupid fucking face," Donut says.

"Some people find my face an image of perfection." Lana swishes away.

"Get over yourself, Donut!" Sam says. "That drunk only had seven dollars. Kit's brought in 12!"

"Does that mean I've passed?" I say.

"Jury's still out." Her look is calculating. "I'll call a house meeting tomorrow. You may as well continue scabbing."

*

Sam, cross-legged on the kitchen cabinet, flicks ash out the window. I can hear the sound of the surf hitting the rocks below the apartment building.

"You've passed," she says. "You can stay."

"Thank you. I'll scab and steal with the best of them, just you watch."

"I will. Now there are rules when you live here. Number one: all dole money is pooled."

"Two… " A scream echoes from the cliffs.

"Two," she continues. "You're forbidden to get a proper job."

Another scream.

"Rule number three." She tosses out the finished fag and drags the window shut. "Stay away from the cliffs."

"Why?"

"It's a gay beat and the Bondi Gang go there to bash poofters. They chase them off the edge."

Another scream, fainter through the glass. I picture the waves, ocean monsters, leaping up and swallowing falling men.

"Should we ring the police?"

"I've tried that. The cops don't do anything. They hate poofters, too."

*

Sam went to school with the Bondi Gang. She'd out-surfed, out-wagged, and out-partied all of them. They bowed to her when she was expelled and were in awe when she was gifted her own apartment. To the Bondi Gang, Sam lived the gilded life. No homework, no parents, and her own place. But they should have checked her bedroom walls before they placed her on a pedestal. The proof of her decadence is there in all its technicolor glory.

Sam loves the Gender-Benders. Her walls are covered in posters of Boy George, Marilyn, and Pete Burns. It's like moving us in is the closest she can do to bring her wall posters to life.

Sam sensed trouble with the Bondi Gang and organised a meeting. Just her and them. I don't know how she did it, but she extracted promises that we could stay. That we would remain untouched if we followed one simple rule: stay away from the cliffs.

The closest we're allowed to go is a little rocky cove at the base where we're permitted to swim unmolested. The dead are often hauled out here, some still clutching strands of hair.

We rarely swim at Bondi Beach. Even with Sam it's too dangerous. There are too many unknowns. Men from outside the area, with whom Sam holds no sway, could encircle and try to drown us. It's hard to fight in water.

.6.

There's a telescope on tripod legs in the apartment that belongs to Sam's father. It's the only possession of his besides the television that Sam hasn't hocked at the pawn shop, and only because she won't get anything near its worth.

Mort carries it out onto the balcony and trains the lens across the valley while the others nap or lounge about flicking through the channels.

Bored one afternoon, I wander out to join him. "What are you looking at?"

"The perfect gay couple." He steps aside like a proud scientist. "Matteo is Italian and 25. Liam's Swedish and 26."

I fit my eye to the eyepiece. "How do you know that?"

He shrugs and I assume it's a made-up story.

I adjust the lens until the mashing colours separate and settle. Red coalesces into a parked sports car, dashes of dark green become fence pickets, brown becomes brick, and fluttering whiteness becomes the curtains sucking in and out of windows as if the townhouse is breathing. Between their folds I spy the curved arms and legs of modern furniture and two young men sprawled on a couch in a mess of cushions. "Is Liam the blond and Matteo the brunet?"

"Yes," Mort says.

"Figures."

"Aren't they adorable?"

"'Spose," I say. "If you like that sort of thing." They look like every fashion-conscious boy on the streets of Sydney. Floppy shiny hair like from a shampoo commercial, white T-shirts and baggy jeans, à la Nick Kamen in the Levi's 501 commercial.

"How do you know they're gay?"

He looks sheepish, "I've seen them do things."

"You sicko," I say admiringly.

"That's not why I watch."

"What then?"

"They're a happy couple," Mort says. "They exist. If happiness can happen for them, it can happen for any of us."

I take another look and focus on the room they are in. Big television, the piles of magazines, nice sofa, art on the walls. Too perfect. Affronted and jealous, I say, "Pfft, I hate them and their cushions."

Mort looks pissed off. "You're like them," he nods at the others lying inside watching *Green Acres* and pulling drags on the last cigarette. "You just want to hate everything."

"Maybe, but at least I'm not investing in a dumb fantasy."

"They exist," he says, exasperated. "They're right there in front of us."

"No." I look him up and down with deliberate cruelty. "What's right in front of me is a pervert."

"Fuck off."

Mort and I refuse to talk to one another for weeks: weeks in which he gets more and more addicted to the telescope. He pretends to have migraines, so he doesn't have to go out scabbing. This angers Sam because Mort and I are her best scabs and his absence is affecting her bottom line.

"If he's not going to scab then he can piss off," Sam says angrily.

"Hock the telescope," Donut says. "Problem solved."

"It'll break his heart," Lana says. "But, if he's not contributing to the haul, it can't be helped."

"It's my dad's telescope so I'll do what I like," Sam says.

I feel sad for our friendship and decide to warn him of his impending loss.

"How're Matteo and Ben?"

"They're ill."

"How ill?"

"They've got the disease."

"How do you know?"

"I read their mail."

"Wow. I didn't think the telescope was that powerful."

He doesn't laugh. "It isn't. I go through their car and letterbox at night, when youse are out scabbing."

"How long has this been going on?"

"Since I first discovered them."

"So, Liam and Matteo are real names?"

He nods.

"Well, you've got to stop. If you don't come out scabbing, Sam's going to evict you."

"I can't," he says, "What if something happens to them while I'm out?"

"You don't know them."

"I do." He's stubborn.

"It's not healthy."

"I know how to care! I'm the healthiest one of all of you! You're the freaks!"

I stalk inside and stand between Sam and the television. "Sell the telescope."

Later, when the others have left for the bottle shop, I hear Mort's gasp on the balcony. I find him bent over as if he's having an asthma attack.

"Are you alright?"

He points to the eyepiece as he sinks to the balcony tiles.

I can't tell what I'm looking at. The curtains breathe in and out, but their bedroom doesn't look right. The shapes and colours coalesce. I focus on the rear of the room. Something large and misshapen is hanging off the back of the door.

Outside, the red sports car skids to a halt. Liam vaults out, inserts the key in the front door lock and throws himself through it. When I see him next he is in the bedroom. *No! No! No!* He seizes the shape about the middle and wrenches it onto the bed. It is Matteo with rope round his neck. Liam is kissing Matteo all over, but Matteo doesn't respond.

Liam walks to the window. His hands claw the curtains out of the air. He holds them like the ropes of a swing.

"No!"

"What?" Mort rasps.

"He threw himself out."

"What do you mean?"

"Liam! Out the window."

Mort clambers up, pushes me aside and gasps before falling away.

I return to the telescope.

The curtains have resumed their breathing. Matteo's corpse lies on the bed. People are exiting their houses and a woman, one hand pressed to her mouth, stands pointing at Liam's body draped over the arrow-heads of the fence, his white tee-shirt turning the same colour as his car.

That's true love, I think.

Later that afternoon Mort decides to go and pay his final respects. I accompany him on the proviso that he'll resume scabbing duties when we return. Dusk falls. We gather flowers from the front yards along the way. Mort leads me to the house. Masked and gloved neighbours are out hosing and bleaching the street. We're eyed suspiciously. The chemical smell is repellent. We drop our flowers at the base of a nearby paperbark tree and return home.

The next day Sam hocks the telescope for nowhere near its true value.

.7.

"What's your name?" he growls, his buffalo nostrils flaring an inch away from my face. The Pied Piper has me pinned me up against the telegraph pole on my scabbing corner. On either side of him, his two blond cohorts flicker like pale wavering flames.

"Kit," I say.

"Fucken Kit! What's that short for?"

"Kitten." I try to act sexy.

"What name's on your birth certificate, ya little whore?" He plunges his face into my throat and nuzzles me like a grizzly.

"Davy," I make it sweet.

"Do you know who I am?" he says.

"The Pied Piper."

His green eyes flash.

"Me name's Bennie and I run a club for gentlemen who'd like the look of *you*. How old are ya?"

I drop two years.

"16."

"Come with me and you'll make more in a night than you'll make all year begging."

"How much?"

"A thousand bucks if you're good," he says. "Fabian? Randy? Ain't that right?"

He backs off and lets his pale flames take the baton. Their cologne smells of burnt orange and caramel. They extend their long swimmer arms to showcase their golden watches. "Rewards for being good."

I'm entranced.

"I can be good."

"That's enough fellas," the Pied Piper chuckles, parting them like curtains. "Let the lad breathe." He places his heavy hand against my hip. "There are rules. Like you gotta lose the stupid fag name and be a real boy."

His fingers reach up. "And you gotta lose this," he says, stroking my rouged cheek. "And this," his fingers knock my earrings. "And this," he runs his index finger beneath my kohl darkened eye.

He wants the boy I left on the Brisbane lino.

I feel the telegraph pole splinters digging into my back. "No thanks."

"Fine." He releases me, suddenly bored. "Be a freak."

"Be a freak," his blonds echo, ponytails swinging like pendulums as they strut away.

Proper boys die. It's the freaks that live.

.8.

The night is hot. I count the fruit bats following the strands of scent into the Botanic Gardens.

"FAGGGGGOOTTTTT!"

Orange Datsun. Young guys hanging out like keystone cops. The one hanging out furthest has blond mullet hair and arm raised with bottle poised to throw.

Glass explodes against the footpath. I hop like a marionette. Red droplets appear on my naked legs from tiny fragments as the car hoons up Oxford Street.

"PRICKKK!" I scream, unable to think of anything harder. Arsehole doesn't roll off the tongue. Oxford Street, for those haters, is a cesspit and its inhabitants walking up and down it are vermin drawn to the smell. It's ironic because they're drawn too but they don't realise. In fact, the longing on some of their faces is obvious. It makes them even more pathetic.

I brush the glass shards from my skin and return to my scabbing duties.

Hoping to leverage any sympathy from a man who must have witnessed the attack, I say, "Excuse me, do you have 20 cents?"

"Get a job."

I shrug and lean against the telegraph pole. "Keep asking," as Sam says. "It's the law of averages. You're bound to win sometimes."

*

Oxford Street is a war zone and the bars are bomb shelters where fingers of mirror-ball light strafe the shell-shocked. People, mainly men, sit at tables in The Mirror Bar staring into the past because the future doesn't exist.

*

After scabbing duty, we position ourselves on the bitumen footpath outside the Exchange and wait for the Japanese tourists who disgorge from tour buses and take our photographs as if we're punks in Trafalgar Square. We follow Sam's rule to the letter and as the tourists pull out their cameras, we put out our hands for money: never give anything away. Not even an image. Sam invests the money in cask wine from the Bottle Shop. She keeps the bladders cool and hidden in the toilet cisterns of the Exchange and sells to the underage kids.

Lana says that a city is just a gang of buildings, and that our gang is Sydney personified. Sam is Centrepoint Tower looking over us all. Toni, Sam's blonde best friend is Australia Square, the white tower closest. Donut is the Harbour Bridge because he is the first Brisbane refugee that Sam took in, and our pathway to her. And, of course, Lana is the Opera House on display for public consumption.

Lana found it hard to find appropriate landmarks for Mort and me, but finally decided on Parramatta Road and the Pacific Highway, bringing in the practical goods. We are the best scabs, and the best thieves. We have to be – we are at the bottom of the pecking order. I just wish I could be something more memorable, but not Luna Park because I don't want to be a clown.

After the Exchange we go to Patchs, the nightclub cross the road, to watch the drag shows. The Sydney drag shows are 10 times better than Brisbane's, and sometimes I see Destiny on stage having come down to fill a spot. She never acknowledges me.

If the drugs are too strong we retreat to the grass of Hyde Park and stare up at Centrepoint Tower as if it's a needle on the record of the turning universe. We make up songs and talk shit about strange phenomena like spontaneous combustion, or parallel universes and how to reach one. Mort's of the opinion that the mad people wandering the streets are simply people who've found their way here from another dimension and the dawning real-isation has made them crazy.

"Even the Opera Lady?" I say.

"Yep. She switched places with her parallel self." Mort sits up as if he's discovered the answer. "She pitches that one note she sings back at her home planet hoping to hear something back."

I still prefer Quoll's version of the Opera Lady.

After regaining our equilibrium, we trudge up to Olympic Yeeros to buy potato scallops – large golden potato coins that we slather with tomato sauce – and head home, piled over each other in a taxi like baby snakes in a red belly's nest.

.9.

The space shuttle Challenger, a teacher onboard to study Halley's Comet, explodes as it roars from Earth. On the television screen the trails left by the falling parts hang like the ropey tendrils of a jellyfish. Hooting and hollering we beat our chests and jump up and down like apes.

The American President Ronald Reagan is on the television. He says there'll be more teachers sent to space.

"Send up the lot of 'em," Sam says with a laugh.

We are cruel, wasteful, useless creatures. The best-of-the-best die while our kind lives on.

But what is this life?

All I want is to fit in. To find a home.

Am I happy?

This life is too hard for happiness.

Am I miserable?

This life is too exciting to be miserable. There's a wildness here and a feeling of possibility that didn't exist in Brisbane.

What I am is hungry.

Through the kitchen window I watch shadowy men move through the night streets on their way to the headland beat. *Stay away from the cliffs where gays go to hunt sex, and where the gang goes to hunt gays.* These men I'm watching aren't like me. They appear like ordinary men with regular jobs risking everything for physical pleasure. I don't look ordinary, don't have a job, and physical pleasure isn't worth putting my life on the line for. I'm the negative to their positive.

My flatmates and I never have sex with one another – we are literally siblings. We have sex with our sugar daddies, the bankers, lawyers and professionals who take us out to dinner, which also means Sam doesn't have to waste money on feeding us. Back in the apartment, we talk about food and what we ate, but never what we did for it.

Lana is taken to the best restaurants and the rest of us are jealous. "Daddy bought me figs wrapped in a special bacon and smothered in blue cheese," he says. "I've never tasted a thing more divine."

"My daddy told me there's a toadfish dish in Japan that can kill you," Mort says. "It's prepared in such a way to make it edible, but you can never be sure when you eat it. It's called fugu."

Sex is like fugu. Eat it and you could die.

Lana's had his daddy the longest and knows all the tricks of the trade. He leans against the doorjamb while I'm getting ready in the bathroom mirror for my date with the French banker. "Rule number one: make sure you get money for the powder room. Two: agree with everything he says. Three: bring home any leftovers. It's how us starlets survive. Four: never, ever, swallow, and I'm not talking tucker."

Frenchie takes me somewhere local and then down to the southern end of the beach to blow me. I hold the doggie bag and try to keep an eye out for the Bondi Gang, my eyes and ears peeled for the subtle variations and changes in atmosphere that's often a precursor to violence. Thanks to my stepfather prepping me with his fists and feet I can read what is going to happen before it happens. I am prescient. I am a seismograph.

Mort's sugar daddy is a medical specialist who takes him out for lamb chops and then back to his place where he peels off Mort's clothes and studies his body as if he's been laid out on a mortuary table. Mort never has to do anything physical, or so he says. Donut is looking for a new daddy. (His old one left him for a younger model.) He's set his sights on Gorgeous George our drug dealer, who deals the sugar that Donut loves best. Scab money, dole money and powder room money are pooled and spent at GG's place.

We file into the ground-floor apartment and make small talk as GG cuts and bags smack and speed in his wheelchair. We flick through his scrapbooks filled with newspaper and magazine cut-outs declaring him the Australian Nureyev. We keep our eyes averted from the torpedo-shaped stump under his woollen blanket.

GG used to be Australia's most promising ballet dancer before he nodded-off on heroin in front of a three-bar-heater with his two beautiful legs intact and woke with just one.

"You all think you're pretty now," he says, idly scratching his phantom limb. "But just you wait."

A frantic knocking on the door. "Be a good boy and open it." Donut does as he's told and a sweating man races in, pulls down his pants and drops to his haunches.

"Say hello to Scooter," GG says. "Scooter's just got back from Thailand."

"Hello Scooter."

Scooter nods and starts to strain.

"Not on the carpet!" GG flaps a black plastic bag at me and motions me to the floor. "Quick, slide this under him and count what comes out."

I do as I'm told. Head against the dirty carpet I watch him squeeze out oily, shit flecked, white balls.

"One," I count. "Two…"

"What does it look like?" Donut says.

"Like a turtle laying eggs."

Laughter. Even Scooter guffaws. Except I'm not laughing. I'm learning a dirty lesson. Sixteen balls later I've promised myself I'll never end up one-legged, or like a laying turtle.

.10.

"There they are motoring home back to the Eastern Suburbs." Quoll waves his hand at the elderly woman and man sitting stiff-backed behind the windows of a black limousine waiting at the traffic lights.

"Who?"

"My parents," he emits a bitter laugh. "Once a week they eat out in the city."

"Do you want me to get their attention?" I step towards the road.

"No." The light turns green. "Neither of them ever looks left or right, despite the fact they know I live up this street."

"Are they rich?"

"Yes, but they're poverty stricken in every other way."

"Bye bye, Mum! Bye bye, Dad!" As the car accelerates away up Oxford Street he jumps up from the gutter and goosesteps madly about the foot-path, chanting in a gruff voice, "Do not raise your hands above chest level. Don't play with your hair like a girl. Stand with your legs apart, not with your legs together. You're not a woman with something to protect. Walk like you've got flippers on your feet. That's how men walk."

He starts to cough and sinks back down to the footpath to catch his breath, "You're lucky you come from nothing."

"I don't come from nothing. If I came from nothing, I'd have nothing," I say. "I've got scars. I couldn't walk for two days after one of my stepfather's beatings, and after another I got stitches."

"You really are a scab, aren't you?" he laughs. Then sees my face. "Oh, I'm sorry. I didn't mean to be rude. Here," he rustles through his jacket, "take this as an apology."

He hands me his silver cigarette case.

"That's not necessary."

"Please, take it off my hands," he says. "It was my father's."

I marvel at the silver patterning. "Tell me if you change your mind."

"I won't change my mind," he says. "Now put it in your pocket and get back to work. Money doesn't grow on trees."

A man walks past in a *Choose Life* T-shirt.

"I hate that slogan," Quoll groans. "If only I could."

The traffic falls quiet and all we can hear is the heartbeat thump, thump, thump of New Order's 'Blue Monday' coming from the Exchange.

Quoll strokes a lesion on his neck. "There's a scientist who reckons the disease was dusted over the planet by a comet's tail."

"First it was Haitian voodoo," I say. "Then swine flu."

"It was a pity about the Challenger," he says. "NASA could've discovered the truth."

I remember how we'd howled, cackled and gibbered as the shuttle exploded. Annihilation. "Do you really think it came from comet dust?"

He shrugs, "Most scientists reckon monkeys."

"Do you wanna hear a joke?" I say.

"No."

"What did the nymphomaniac say to the necrophiliac?"

"What?" he sighs.

"Fuck me dead!"

"My ashes are going to be scattered like a comet's tail," he says, ignoring the punchline. "It's all arranged. You'll see."

*

I help Quoll to his apartment. He lives on the 12th floor.

"Please come in," he says formally and sees me hesitate. "Don't get the wrong idea," he says. "I like my men to look like men."

I help him in and settle him on the couch. There are photos of his dead architect boyfriend on all the tables and framed detailed plans of Centrepoint on the walls. His boyfriend was handsome in that clone sort of way.

Quoll sees me looking at his dead lover.

"Do you know grief?" he says.

I shake my head, "I don't think so. Not yet anyway."

"You will. He's an indiscriminate bastard."

He gets up and pulls the curtains to reveal Centrepoint glittering like a night-time sun. "That's all I have to do to see my baby's greatest achievement shining bright."

.11.

"The cops found another body on the rocks," Mort races in from the shop with a fresh packet of fags. "They're saying it's suicide. Who's coming to investigate?"

"Bullshit it's suicide." Donut inhales his fresh durrie like his life depends on it. "How flat's the water?"

"Like a pond," Mort says. "We can swim if you want."

Lana's dozing on the couch. Donut blows smoke into his face. "Wake up."

I give Sam a shake. "You coming?"

"Na, I'm too hungover. Just make sure you stay away from the cliffs," she reminds us.

"We're just going to explore where the body landed, not do the beat," Mort admonishes.

We play dress-ups to visit death. We drape ourselves in long strands of plastic beads, knot lengths of material about our waists, and hang diamantes from our lobes. Lana paints a quick face and unfolds a painted Chinese umbrella.

The stone of South and North Bondi is the colour of a dingo's paws and Bondi Beach is cradled between them. It's hot and the South Bondi rock shelf stinks of rotting seaweed. An old man stands on the rock shelf scanning the cliff face. The body has been removed. Clouds of flies rise as he moves away. "It's not where I'd jump," he says.

"He didn't jump." Donut watches the departing figure. "He was chased off."

Lana gazes down at the congealing puddles of blood. "I wonder who he was?"

"Some poor bugger," Donut says.

"Should we say a prayer?" Mort says.

Lana says, "Now I lay me down to sleep, I pray the Lord my soul to keep,

If I should die before I wake, pray the Lord my soul to take."

"That's for little kids," Donut says.

Lana shrugs. "It's the only one I know. Mumma used to say it every night as she tucked me in under my duvet in Chinchilla."

Mort laughs. "You had a duvet made out of chinchilla?"

"No, silly," Lana says. "I grew up in Chinchilla. It's an outback town."

"Wherever you originated, your Mumma wouldn't have been praying for *your* soul," Donut drawls. "She'd have been praying for a brand-new child!"

Lana swings the umbrella at him.

"My Mumma loves me just the way I am."

"Just like all our mothers," Mort laughs.

A wave churns up over the hot rock shelf. We watch it fizz and pop, scatter flies, and greedily pull the blood back into the ocean.

We clamber back to the little cove, submerge ourselves in all our finery and float over boulders covered in emerald weed. Turning and twisting I let myself sink to the bottom and wonder at the man's terror as he fell.

We stay in till the water becomes too choppy.

A shout of "FAGGOTS!" stabs our backs as we make our way back up the slope. We rotate on our heels like well-oiled machinery.

Below, on the headland track, the insult thrower stands over his dropped pushbike. Salt glitters in his blond hair, and his upper lip is snagged in a sneer over a reef of white teeth. He holds a can of drink and the front spokes of his bike spin like a roulette wheel. His bare feet are covered in sand.

Six disciples stand behind him in the mangle of their dropped bikes. The youngest looks about 12.

The Bondi Gang, part thereof, returning to the scene of the crime. They stare up at us like seagulls.

If Sam was here, she'd know all these boys by name. But she stayed home.

We're outnumbered but strangely unperturbed as if the death of one of our own has encased us in invincibility.

"You called?" Donut angles a naked leg through his sarong and gives them an eyeful.

Mort, hands on hips, purses his lips and says, "Tell us something we don't know."

"Honey," Lana, twirls his umbrella. "We're the biggest fags you've ever seen."

I say, "You made a deal with Sam. We're allowed to swim here."

The spinning pushbike wheel comes to a stop.

"I don't *deal* with faggots."

The thug hurls his drink and misses. I know his face. He's the guy from the orange Datsun who threw the bottle. A sweet orange smell fills the air as Fanta fizzes out over the loose gravel at the tips of Lana's painted toes. Gravel and stones. Pay dirt. We are standing on a field of missiles. Lana clicks his tongue. It's the sound of the roulette ball finding its slot.

We whir into action.

Rat-a-tat-tat. Howling, bending, throwing, machine gun dervishes we rain down stones. The gang is trapped on the path in the mangle of their bikes. They scream and shout, contort like contestants in a '50s dance-a-thon. The baby of the pack takes a rock to the face and collapses sobbing over the frames.

The leader cries. "Stop!"

"Who's the fag now?" Donut aims another rock at the youngest boy who, still snivelling, holds onto the blond's arm. It's obvious they're brothers.

"I am," the blond seethes.

"You said it!" Donut yells.

Extricating themselves from their bikes the gang members blunder back the way they came. "Youse are dead meat!" the blond cries over his shoulder.

Word of the proclamation filters back: we're to be bashed on sight. Wherever. Whenever. It's impossible to leave the apartment looking the way we do or we'll be caught. Returning to Queensland seems a distinct possibility.

.12.

I believe we were baptised when we swam in that murdered man's blood. He couldn't save himself, so he saved us instead. Within a week of the rock-throwing incident Sam's father puts the apartment on the market and tells her she has to move out. Sam's the only one with any money. We don't stand a chance without her.

We remove all our jewellery, scrub our faces, and dye our hair brown. We dress in boring clothes and practise using our real names to visit real estate agents.

The only place anyone will rent us is a tiny cold dump backing onto six sets of train tracks on the opposite side of the city. Deep in the heart of skinhead territory. Now, instead of the ocean we hear the cold roar of trains. Now, instead of sunlight we live in permanent shadow. Now, instead of ozone we smell the trains' vented air and oil on the tracks. Erskineville is a world away from Bondi but at least here the gang won't find us, and at least we'll no longer hear the cliff-top screams.

Every morning, heading to the backyard loo, I see trains big as ocean waves stalled at the back fence waiting for the signal to roll into the city. Office workers with dead faces stare down from the yellow windows as if from inside a whale's eye.

*

Fever, night sweats, swollen glands. Is it a cold, the flu, or the gay plague? I count the times bodily fluids could have entered my blood stream. Counting is useless when we don't even know if it can spread by kissing. My health is crap: the Erskineville house is cold and damp, my diet's abysmal, too much drugs and alcohol.

At first, only gays and I.V. drug users were being killed. I'm bundled up in blankets on the couch when the ad appears on television.

Only? I say to myself. Did I hear that correctly? These victims are unimportant. Nothing to get too upset over.

A sweet blonde child clutches a doll to her chest. There's a lot of fake smoke. The doll goes flying.

But now we know every one of us can be devastated by it.

The fact is, over 50,000 men, women, and children now carry the virus, but in three years nearly 2000 of us will be DEAD. If not stopped it could kill more Australians than World War Two.

If you have sex have just one safe partner, or always wear condoms.

Always.

In the ad there is no heaven for the stricken, not even the children. They are bulldozed off the edge into an abyss as if into the pits of hell.

The atmosphere of death, disaster, and disease thickens over Oxford Street like shellac. You need special shoes for this bowling alley. Steel capped for head kicking, and, if you're a skinhead red shoelaces, that means you love to fight.

We gays are presented as being the official Grim Reapers aiming our balls at all the innocent straights. Every thug in a 50 kilometre radius thinks it's their duty to come see how many faggots they can knock down. They hoon up the street in hot rods hanging out their windows flinging all manner of verbal and literal shit. Bashings increase tenfold. Not only do we have the Bondi Gang and skinheads to watch out for, now we also have armies of outraged suburbanites to contend with.

My cough worsens. I spit phlegm. This is it. I know I've got it. I can't wait any longer. I make my way to Dr Edelsten's 24-hour clinic on Broadway where the neon sign "You have never been treated so well" greets me at the front door. It's the most beautiful surgery in the world. Chandeliers, potted palms, a white baby grand, and mink covered examination tables. It's all bulk-billed. There is one other patient in the waiting area, a muttering mad old woman with her face bent close to the television showing scenes from the funeral of Anna Gatt whom that day was buried in one of the longest funeral processions Sydney has ever seen. The camera shows the Gatt matriarch's husband and son walking slowly behind the black wagonette escorting the body to Mortuary Station and then on to its final resting place at Rookwood Cemetery. Then come some advertisements including the Grim Reaper.

The old woman turns hissing from the television, "Death is coming, and he has a counting system. Tinker, tailor, soldier, sailor, rich man, poor man, beggar man," her finger points at me. "THIEF!"

I look for help. The receptionist intones, "Please don't harass our patients, Mrs Abraham. If you can't behave, I'll have to ask you to leave."

The old woman stabs her finger at the receptionist. "And the girl over there who salts the beef!"

The receptionist comes around to escort her to the door. The old woman rants, "You're all next! You're all next!"

It's an omen.

"Yes, Mrs Abraham," the receptionist says. "We're all next. All of us. Death is a part of life."

But when I die, I think, I won't be wheeled down the street in a glass-sided, glossy black wagonette.

The doctor calls my name.

I'm laid out on the mink table and examined. I must remember to tell Lana. She grew up in Chinchilla.

I only have bronchitis. I'm given a script.

.13.

Destiny's in town 'guest-starring' at the Exchange. It's a windless night and from my scabbing corner I can hear her on stage yelling into the microphone.

"Have you seen that Grim Reaper?" she yells. "He's wearing a feed bag for Christ's sake. Tell him to piss off to Zink & Sons! And what's with that name? He needs a drag name. And alliteration is everything when it comes to drag names! Rhonda Reaper! Not very catchy though, but who wants to catch that?"

The Grim Reaper's in the audience laughing louder than anyone. He can take a joke and he might even go and check out Zink & Sons.

Sam's warning whistle rends the night air. Something's coming. I run to the cement traffic island and scan the street. I see it. A centipede races up from the bowels of the city. I hear their tread.

A drunk sways under a streetlight. It's Quoll. He's not drunk, he's sick. He steps onto the road to cross to the safety of the Exchange. He's seen the skinheads, he will escape in time. I'm relieved.

Ooooooooooo. The Opera Lady releases her call and Quoll halts in his tracks. He gazes in her direction. His eyes find mine. I call out to him to run but he steps back onto the footpath. His arms flail as the centipede encircles him and he falls beneath the artillery strikes of their black shiny boots. Quoll feeds their blood lust, so they'll have less to dish out to the singing woman, and me. A sob escapes my throat. There is nothing I can do.

Patrons pour out of the Exchange like bull ants from a disturbed nest. Lana Pellay is singing 'Pistol in my Pocket'. Rent boys unfurl their studded belts and coil them about their fists. Dykes swing their keys like truncheons. Destiny seethes, "I fucken hate skinheads," slips off her high heels and wields them like scythes. She sees me extract my box-cutter. "Don't be a dickhead," she says, acknowledging me for the first time. "Put the knife away."

We fan out and surround the kicking, spitting, centipede, which hasn't posted a lookout because it thinks it's impregnable.

Destiny, leading the charge, swings her high heel at the head of the leader. The rent boys and dykes dive in, attacking tooth and claw, our wild keening undercutting the skinheads' roar, our assault making them dumb. The centipede falls about segmented, confused, fear on each face as they flee. But they leave behind one of their own. I grind my boot in his face. Destiny screams, *We are not victims. We are warriors!* It's a field day. My box-cutter is unnecessary, the kicking enough. The skin's arms and legs snap.

Quoll is carried back to the bar, but the skinhead remains lying on the footpath.

When a skinhead's skull bleeds there's no hair to soak up the blood and it spurts and runs in dazzling rivulets. The revenge bashing only stops with the approach of the Opera Lady. She glides by without a sound. She doesn't want his soul.

.14.

"Did you miss me?" Quoll extends a closed fist. Coin-sized copper lesions sit on the back of his hand like a magician's coin trick.

"Dreadfully."

He releases the real coins and they drop like pennies from heaven.

"That's why I discharged myself," he says. "To put you out of your financial misery."

"Are you alright?"

"Of all the men in my ward I'm the only one still alive. So yes."

"Your number's not up yet," I say.

"At least the nurses fed me this time," he sighs. "When I was first diagnosed, they'd leave the food tray out in the corridor and make me crawl for it."

Quoll seems gratified by my shock. He settles in on the footpath with his boots in the gutter. I remember Mort's theory about how a head knock might be enough to push someone into a parallel universe.

"Does everything look the same to you now you're out of hospital?" I say.

"The same abysmal mess of tortured lives and dashed hopes?" he says, wryly. "Sure, why not?"

A silver bus rolls into the bay across the road. The street is washed with waves of exhaust. We watch the passengers disgorge.

"Oxford Street is a zoo just like Taronga," Quoll holds his fingers over his face and stares at me through the gaps. "Scavengers, predators, and prey. Spiders, cheetahs, hyenas. They rush the bars. Some will take your hand off, some will lick, others will cover you in piss."

I strike a pose. "What animal am I? Predator, scavenger, or prey?"

"That's too obvious."

I jingle the coins in my pocket. "Scavenger?"

"Bingo," he says.

His laugh turns into a coughing fit. I pat his back and feel the knuckles of his spine beneath the material of his jacket.

The disembarked passengers hoist luggage and are siphoned away in taxis and cars.

"Pretty boy." Quoll points at a boy wearing a red beanie standing on the footpath like something forgotten. "Another runaway come to the big smoke."

"What makes you think he's a runaway?"

"Worldly belongings in one bag. Big jacket. Hat pulled down. No one to meet him," he says. "I've seen a hundred just like him. This world will eat him up."

"He'll cope," I say.

"He's our Bambino. We saw him first, and we must keep an eye on him. You must keep an eye on him."

"Why can't you?"

"You know why," he lifts a spindly arm. "We're only allotted a certain number of days and I'm running out of mine. Come, help me up."

I hoist him to his feet. He searches his pockets, holds out his hand.

"You've already paid!" I say.

He drops the coins into my palm. "This is for our Bambino. Promise me you'll give it to him. He'll need all the help he can get."

I deposit Bambi's money into a different pocket to the one which holds my beggings.

"Promise," I say.

"Night Scab."

"Night Quoll."

He shuffles off into the gloom of Riley Street.

The night is cold. Bambino, hugging his bag, folds himself down against the bus terminal wall.

An hour passes. I scab a couple of dollars.

Sam's whistle shatters the cold. I dash out to the traffic island to scan for the threat and spot the centipede scuttling up from the city. I've got time

83

to run back to the Exchange but then I remember my promise to Quoll. I rush to the boy. "We've got to hide!"

Startled, he looks up through two swollen black eyes.

"Why?"

"Centipede."

He looks at me uncomprehending.

"Skinheads." I stare at his damaged face.

He snatches up his bag and follows without a word.

We duck up the lane and crouch behind some bins to the scuff of marching boots.

"They'll beat the shit out of us if they find us," I whisper.

Two of them enter the laneway. I raise my finger to my lips. The skinheads undo their flies and piss against the wall.

They shake their dicks and jog back out. The smell of piss mingles with the garbage smell.

The boy squints at me through bruised eyes, "That was lucky."

"It looks like somebody's already had a go at you," I say.

"My stepdad," he says.

I'm even more intent on saving him.

"What's your name?" I say.

"Nathan," he says.

"You'll need a camp name."

"What's that?"

"A mask you hide behind. But you can't choose your own. It has to be bestowed."

"I'll try anything," he grins.

"Turn and face me," I say. I lower an invisible sword down on each shoulder. "I baptise you Bambi."

"I'm not Bambi!" he says, raising his voice. "I'm not a fucking girl!"

"Bambi was a boy!" I say. "Didn't you see the movie?"

"I don't care!" He clambers to his feet.

"Ssshh." I pull him down. "You'll get us killed."

I recall my humiliation when Destiny bestowed my camp name: Kitten, Kitty, Kit. The silly names that make us sound like walking jokes. But it's black humour and black humour can be an effective ointment for our ills.

Sam whistles the all-clear. We dust ourselves off and return to my corner. Lana swishes up the street. He's a vision in head-to-toe leopard print and his hair is done-up like the boy singer Marilyn's.

"Sam wants to know how much you've scabbed," Lana says.

Bambi is looking at him as if Lana's repellent and it hasn't escaped Lana.

"What's up bruiser's nose?" he says.

"This is Bam…" The boy gives me a fierce look. "This is Nathan. He's a runaway. Do you think he can stay at our place?"

"There's no room," Lana says flatly.

The boy looks relieved.

Lana takes my scabbings and heads back to Sam.

"Don't worry about me," Nathan says. "I can look after myself."

"Here," I say, extracting my box-cutter from my boot and handing it over. "Just in case."

I show him how the blade slides in and out of its casing.

I show him how to scab. I recall all of Sam's rules and relay them one by one. Or, I think I do.

When my scabbing shift's done, I lead him down to the Exchange but the bouncers refuse to let him in because of his black eyes.

"I'll go find us a drink," I say. "You'll be fine. You've got the knife. Here's something else," I hold out Quoll's deposit. "Take this."

"I don't want your money," he says.

"It's not mine," I say, trying to find the right word. "It's from a benefactor."

I leave him sitting on the front step. I leave him too long. When I return – drink in hand, two straws – I see a flash of red in a cab pulling away. His beanie. A man's thick iridescent arm rests along the back of the seat like a fat python. I thought I'd told him all of Sam's Rules, but I'd forgotten the most important. Beware the Pied Piper.

.15.

Life shifts gears as it's prone to do. Sam tells us she's sick of Erskineville and misses the beach and her father's generosity. She's returning to Bondi. The lease is signed over to Mort and me and Sam says we can keep the bond money.

The Queen is dead. Long live the Queens.

Any money I scab is now mine.

.16.

A clanging sound.

A group of men, some masked and harnessed, and others – the Sisters of Perpetual Indulgence – dressed in nuns' habits, exit the Midnight Shift. One nun rings a bell while another begins to swing a brass metal container on three long chains. It dispenses flicks of grey powder.

The procession stops when it gets to my scabbing corner. The bell tongue falls silent.

A masked man steps forward. He has eyes of an incredible green. "Brendan said to give you this."

He holds out a 50 dollar note.

"Who's Brendan?"

"You called him Quoll."

"Where is he?"

"Here." The man motions to the dust that zebra stripes the black bitumen footpath. "We're scattering his ashes up and down Oxford Street."

Comet dust.

The bellringer starts to clang. The procession moves on.

I stuff the 50 into my boot and try to pretend nonchalance, but it's no use.

Muscular arms constrict my rib cage until I can't breathe. Skinhead? 'Bondi' – the thug gang leader from the cliffs? Grim Reaper? No. It's Grief, in human form.

He whispers in my ear. "Are you grieving Quoll?"

I nod.

"Why?" he sneers. "You didn't really know him. He was just a guy you scabbed from on the street. You didn't even know his real name. You're such a fraud."

It's as Quoll said, "Grief's an indiscriminate bastard."

"Leave me alone," I hiss. "What are you even doing here?"

"I love Sydney," he says. "Harbour. Beaches. Sunsets. Best of all I love the different types of woe. A flavour for every occasion! I even enjoy the stupid kind you emit – that doesn't even know what it's grieving."

My mind flops about for an answer but is swamped in panic.

I take deep, slow, breaths, and stare out into the Oxford Street traffic.

Grief will become enamoured by someone else soon. Someone else feeling more loss than me. I turn to tell him to piss off, but he's already evaporated. Nothing but a hollowness remains.

I stare down at Quoll's ashes on the footpath. Pedestrians are trampling on him. I drop to my knees and scrape what I can into his cigarette case.

.17.

The night is young. Drunk, I swing on a No Stopping sign. Bowie's 'Let's Dance' echoes up the street from the Exchange Hotel.

A car pulls up.

"Have you seen my son?"

A woman emerges and extends a photo of a boy sitting before a birthday cake dotted with candles. Even without his black eyes I recognise him.

"That's Bambino," I tuck the newspaper in my back pocket and swing round the pole.

"Bambino? His name's Nathan."

"Maybe in your world."

I remember what Bambino said about his parents. I peer into the car and see the white knuckled fists that gave him the black eyes clenched to the steering wheel. I remember Sam's rule about never giving anything away. Not one iota.

"It'll cost," I say over the engine noise.

The Oxford Street wind fidgets her auburn hair. "How much?"

"20."

"Cents?" she says dumbly.

I shouldn't be scabbing drunk, but Sam's gone so fuck her rules.

"Bucks!" Shock on the woman's face but she clicks open her purse and hands me the red and orange note. I should have tried 50.

"Your son is at the Pied Piper's brothel," I say. "All the Piper's other boys have got the gay plague and he's the fresh meat."

The colour drains from her face. She stares past me for a long moment and then lowers herself back into the car.

"I told you," the man yells. "Are you happy now? Close the fucking door!"

I do her the honours and the vehicle roars away.

.18.

Donut is dead. Overdose in the Cross. We don't know for weeks. He just vanished like so many do these days. The government disposed of his body. No funeral, nothing. Another dead junkie found in an abandoned building.

Lana's gone full-blown woman minus the chop and has been ensconced in her own little inner-city flat courtesy of her loaded sugar daddy. He's even been paying her doctor's bills.

Now it's just Mort and me living in the Erskineville terrace. Mort has turned religious and has covered his bedroom walls in crucifix drawings. He mumbles a lot about returning to Brisbane.

No friggin' way.

Life here is like being a pawn on a board game with Gilligan's Island, Bondi Beach, the Pied Piper's brothel, and Centrepoint, dotted round the edges. Roll the dice, move a square: be beaten by skinheads. Roll the dice, move a square: find a gang to run with. Roll the dice, move a square: be chased off the Bondi cliffs. Roll the dice, move a square: find a Bondi penthouse to live in. Roll the dice, move a square: earn 50 dollars scabbing. Roll the dice, move a square: find a friend. Roll the dice, move a square: catch the disease. Roll the dice: die.

.19.

A young bloke, a labourer, drops one and two cent coins into my outstretched palm. I count his measly offering.

Seven cents. Memory floods back and I'm right back at the beginning. It's what was earned an eon ago on the lino 'per-drink-server'. Snakes and Ladders!

"Cheapskate!" I fling the coins up the roadway. They ping and fly. The guy doesn't look back.

"Prick!" I screech.

He keeps walking.

"Cheapskate shit-for-brains!"

My voice shuttlecocks between the buildings. Pedestrian heads swivel. His too. Eyes and mouth set, he retraces his steps.

In the distance I hear the Opera Lady launch a boat. "*Ooooooooooo.*"

He's upon me. I no longer have the box-cutter. Bambi has it.

POW. POW. POW. My head smacks the bitumen. Time stops.

The Opera Lady sings, "*Oooooooooo.*" Her shimmering golden polyps of sound reverberate. They *are* craft. Spirits line the street, happy and laughing. The disease no longer marks them. In orderly queues they climb into the cages of a huge Ferris wheel that becomes a vast turning galaxy. The carriages lift away. Quoll approaches. He is smiling. His eyes are an incredible blue. His back is straight. He has no trouble walking. He looks just how he looked when I saw him on the television years ago at the opening of Centrepoint. He gazes kindly down.

"Are you alright?" a familiar voice.

Quoll evaporates.

I open my eyes. I haven't seen Ty since Terminus days.

"Man," he says. "You've gotta get a job!"

Three

.1.

After dinner, for the first time, Frenchie takes me back to his city apartment. "I know a cocktail bar looking for a waiter," he says. "The staff each make $100 a night in tips."

That's impossible. This isn't America.

"It's in the basement of that hotel on the corner of Oxford Street and Liverpool, down some footpath stairs. That joint where they serve drinks with real gold."

I know exactly where it is because the stairs are where we used to dump stolen bags.

"I'll write you a reference," Frenchie smirks. "Let them know you give good customer service."

He slides open the roof of his antique rolltop desk and pulls out pen and paper.

"But I haven't any experience," I say as Frenchie drafts the letter.

"They want someone dumb they can train to their own specifications." He hands me the folded paper. "Ask for Andy Flanagan. He owns the place."

.2.

The Burdekin sits wedged like a ship's prow into the crutch of Oxford and Liverpool streets. Full steam ahead and it would've crushed Hyde Park's Emden Gun and slammed into the War Memorial.

Two men compete for an audience in a yelling competition.

"GRID IS GOD'S PUNISHMENT OF THE WICKED! "REPENT! REPENT!" yells the one outside the Westpac Bank.

From atop a milk crate on the opposite side the other bellows "GRID CANNOT BE CAUGHT FROM MOSQUITOES. IT'S GOVERNMENT PROPAGANDA! I AM AN ENTOMOLOGIST BUT LOST MY JOB BECAUSE I WON'T CONFORM TO THEIR LIES!"

The government wouldn't lie about something like that, I think. They're both nuts.

I head down Liverpool Street, descend the footpath stairs, and see the Gold Bar sign painted above a door.

I check my reflection in the window of a fancy cream and burgundy car parked against the curb. Bleached hair swept back and gelled, understated stud earring, smart jacket and tie, manila folder with Frenchie's reference. "You'll do," I say.

"Well look what the cat dragged in," says a guy gnawing on an apple on the other side of the vehicle. Hat pushed back, dirty blond fringe, wearing some kind of uniform. It's Johnnie Minotaur. First, I left Queensland, then Ty, now Johnnie.

"What are you doing here?"

"Well I was sitting on the running board eating my lunch." He wrenches another bite. "You?"

I thumb the bar. "I'm here for a job interview."

"Small world," he smiles. "I'm Andy Flanagan's chauffeur."

I recollect his prior profession. "How'd you score that?"

"You know what they say," he laughs. "It's not what you know…"

The distant town hall clock strikes five.

"Time for my interview," I say.

"Andy Flanagan's a good guy. Good luck."

The Gold Bar is an irregular shaped room tiled in mottled yellow edged by thin bands of dark green. The whole space is illuminated by late afternoon light falling through a large window of opaque glass. Jazz plays quietly to a collection of empty tables and chairs. It looks too austere to be a cocktail bar. On the far side of the room, beside the bar, a doorway opens onto red carpet.

A man and a woman stand working behind the bar counter. Both have jet black hair and pale skin. The man wears a tux and concentrates on a cutting board. The woman, in a purple cocktail dress, polishes a champagne flute with a white cloth.

Behind them the silver-framed glass shelves glow in a soft pink light that picks out the jewel-like tones of the pretty bottles, making them look like exotic birds in an aviary. Greens, yellows, and rubies. Glowing bottles of brown and amber scotch squat on the top shelf like bantam hens.

I descend the short flight of stairs. The woman looks up and says something to the man. He lifts his head and, holding the knife, pushes his glasses up the bridge of his nose with the knuckle of his middle finger. They watch me cross the tiles.

"I'm Kit." I put my hand forward. "I'm here for the job interview."

"Nic." The man puts the knife down and gives my hand a firm shake. "And this is my sister, the Countess."

Her hand is cool.

The man has been cutting gold leaf into small batons that look like little bars of sunlight on the chopping board.

"What are you making?" I say as he deposits them into a container using a brush.

"Gold twists." He places the knife down. "Do you know what a free pour bar is?"

"No."

"We use no measuring devices." Lifting a bottle from the shelves he places it in front of me, his hand resting on its neck. A silver spout like a bird's beak points skyward. It's only a funnel pourer.

I survey the bottles on the shelves. No drink servers. It feels like an omen, but I can't work out if it's good or bad.

"A good barman has to be three things," Nic says. "An acrobat, a diplomat, and a doormat."

I can be an acrobat. I remember the gymnastics of escaping my stepfather's fists. I can be a diplomat. I'm very diplomatic on the street and an expert at turning the other cheek. I can be a doormat. I think of my mother telling us to sit over the holes in the lino.

"I can be all three," I say.

"If you get the job, you'll first learn to be a waiter," the Countess says. "The best waiter is what parents wish from their children – seen and not heard."

"I was raised on that motto."

"A good waiter, Nic says, "is been and gone before the customer even realises."

Like a thief, I think.

"Have you ever carried a drinks tray?" the Countess says. "You'll be of no use if you're not able."

"I learn quickly." This interview isn't going as expected. I fumble for my reference from Frenchie. "I was told to ask for Andy Flanagan."

"It's us you'll be working with." She plucks the folder from my hand and deposits it unopened under the bar. "Follow me. Andy will be down in a minute."

"Table One is our best table," she indicates the corner table closest to the bar. Leading me to the other side of the room, she says, "This is Table 11. Siberia. Take a seat."

I know this game. I settle in as if I've come home.

She gauges me approvingly. "A good waiter has to be humble."

She hands me the folded menu. "You'll have to memorise this."

I recognise very little.

"All our cocktails, despite their golden enhancement, are classics," Countess says, crossing her arms. "So no Sex on the Beach."

She looks at me as if she knows what I've done for a meal.

"Any questions?"

"What's gomme syrup?"

"Sugar water."

I want to ask, why not just call it sugar water? but don't dare.

"What work have you done before?" she says.

Scabbed, stole drinks, and took money from mothers looking for lost sons.

"Factory work," I say, "Assembly line stuff."

"How old are you?" she says.

"18," I say. "You?"

"Never ask a woman her age," she says, as if marking a mental scorecard. "But since you have, what's your guess?"

"28?" I say.

"Close."

"How close?"

"On the right side of close."

"Phew." I fan my face. She smiles and the ice breaks.

"Do you have any questions?" she says.

"Why do people drink gold?"

"Gold is thought to prolong life. Ancient societies like the Egyptians ingested it because it doesn't rust. Also, our customers are filthy rich and like to show off. Who are we to deny them?"

A man wearing a sky-blue suit enters from the internal doorway closest to the bar. The sharp peaks of a folded white handkerchief ornament his jacket pocket. His boyish air is betrayed by the weakened skin about his eyes. I guess early 40s. He stops and speaks with Nic.

"That's Andy," the Countess drops her voice to a whisper. "Listen. You'll do. Take my advice and remove your silver earring and tell Andy you'll stop bleaching your hair."

She is like no one I've ever met. Rude, aloof, mysterious, and friendly. It's only because I like her that I take the stud out of my ear. I've decided already that I don't want to be a doormat and don't want this job. I'll hear what Andy has to say, then go back to doing what I was doing.

As I slip the earring into my jacket pocket my hand bumps Quoll in his cigarette case. I stroke him with an affectionate finger. His voice says, you need this job.

*

"Let's walk," Andy Flanagan leads me out of the bar, across the red carpet, and to the base of a flight of stairs.

"You'll have to carry cocktails on a tray up these to the restaurant," he says.

I look up through the four flights of the building, "Where's the restaurant?"

"At the top," he says. "There's a lift, but it's too ancient and rickety to transport drinks on a tray."

On the next landing, besides the staircase, there are three doors. Through the one closest – door number one – I can hear the men outside yelling on their soapboxes.

"The entomologist gets my vote," Andy says.

"Poor man lost his job," I say. "Would the government lie about insects though?"

"If it would keep them in power," Andy says pushing open the third door to reveal an area dominated by scaffolding and old painters' tarps. The workmen are packing up for the day.

"The entire building, except for the Gold Bar and the restaurant, is undergoing renovation. This will be the new Public Bar. Ciao, Davido! Ciao Richard and Ian! Ciao Andrew, Mike, Jas, James!" Andy calls.

"Cheers Mr Flanno," come the workmen's hearty replies. "See you tomorrow!"

Closing that door, Andy slides open the second. A black grill gate concertinas open onto an elevator that is little bigger than a cupboard. Varnished brown and black walls, capped with a caramel-coloured roof, combined with the red-carpeted floor create a feeling of walking into a layered dessert.

"This old lift is the heart of the hotel," Andy says.

I remember my childhood dream of hiding in a cardboard box and being delivered to Maxim's, La Scala, or the Waldorf. There are no drink servers in the Gold Bar because this bar has been waiting for me. I *am* the drink server.

"I'll never bleach my hair again," I promise.

"Good," Andy says. "Natural is best."

There are five bakelite buttons in the lift. Ground, First, Second, Third, and Fourth. The Fourth requires a key.

Andy Flanagan hits the third, "Besides carrying drinks, the successful applicant's other duty will be to accompany diners to the restaurant."

The lift lurches into action. It cranks past the first and second floor and through the lift window I see more workmen finishing for the day.

"There are rules if you work here," Andy says. "Number one, Nic is master of the bar and Countess is mistress of the customers. Two, you must become master of the menial. Consider the bar a petrol station and the customers cars with their engines running. You must be the boy who ducks out from the garage to pick up any rubbish and wipe down the windscreens."

"Like Johnnie?"

"You know Johnnie?"

"We're both from Brisbane."

"Well that's a coincidence," Andy says. "Now, any questions?"

The lift grinds to a halt.

"What's on the fourth floor?"

"My apartment which is off-limits to customers and staff." He slides open the doors. We exit onto a polished wooden floor. A skylight decorated with winding vines glows above us. I spot a face with intense green eyes watching me through the foliage. A workman on the roof? The face retreats, as if the owner is surprised at being sprung.

Andy Flanagan stands before a large glass door that opens into a long thin rectangular room with two rows of white tables positioned on the diagonal. Three uniformed waitresses in crisp black and white move about placing cutlery. It's what I imagine a train's first-class dining carriage would look like.

"Here, before this restaurant door, is where you will deliver your tray of drinks at the end of your probation," he says. "You have one month and then you will be tested. If you spill one drop on the journey from bottom to top, we'll have to let you go."

.3.

The barber waves me to a seat where there's a folded newspaper left by a previous customer. I'm third in line so open the paper while I wait.

Die, Faggot, Die, screams the headline.

Bullseye. The shock is immediate but I'm paranoid enough to limit the shockwaves showing on my face. In case the folded paper is a test and all those around me are waiting for me to reveal myself. I casually run my eye down the story about the man who donated blood without knowing what he was really donating. I turn the page casually and bury myself in the inquest into the mysterious death of the teenage son of the deputy leader of the Hygiene Party, whose body had been found decomposing on the outskirts of the city.

"What'll it be?"

"Number one all over." I fold the paper and leave it just the way I'd found it. "So it can grow back completely natural."

My bleached hair drops to the floor. White on white. The barber brushes my shoulders and unswirls the cloak from about me as if he's a matador. I feel raw and defenceless. My ears and teeth look gargantuan. My past stares right back at me in the mirror. I can see the imprint of my stepfather's punches and kicks in the back of my eyes. The kicked dog in every fag. The kid back on the lino. It doesn't feel like a fresh start at all.

Oxford Street is full of waiters heading to work. At Taylor Square, people in their vehicles look straight through me. I am just one in an army of servants. Just another drink server. Just a man on the street. Once, at least one of them, would have smirked or mouthed *faggot* through the glass. That lack of recognition should be a good thing, but it makes me feel invisible. Like nothing.

My first task is to crank open the large opaque window to allow in fresh air. Second is to take down all the chairs that have been put on the tables by the cleaners. Third, I place ashtrays on every table and fold the napkins ensuring the creases and angles of each are exact and crisp as Andy Flanagan's white pocket handkerchief.

Nic's in charge of the gold. At the beginning of each shift he dismantles and cleans the special grinder he uses to dispense the flakes into the cocktails. Then he settles down to hand-cut the fine gold leaf into the little bars he'll twist into spirals for martinis.

.4.

The phone rings. I bury my head in my pillow. A train rumbles past and the whole house trembles. The fact the phone is still connected is a surprise. No bills have been paid. Donut is dead, Lana's ensconced in her Taylor Square love nest, and, according to his letter left alongside the Final Notices, Mort's fled back to Brisbane. His room is empty. All his crosses are gone.

The ringing stops and starts. Not even the real estate would be this persistent.

"Hello."

"Auf wiedersehen. Arrivederci. Baai baai!" Lana's voice.

"What?"

"Papi is taking me overseas for my operation," she whispers. "It's all arranged."

"Are you sure about the op?"

"I've never been so sure of anything in my life."

"When are you leaving?"

"Tonight."

"Well, good luck," I say. "You're not the only one with good news."

"Are you getting the chop too?" she laughs.

"I got a job at Andy Flanagan's."

"Well look at us evolving! Hey, do you wanna mind my place? I mean, you can pay me a bit of rent, right?"

"You're a life-saver," I say. "I'm about to be evicted."

"Come visit, I'll give you the key."

*

Kill the fags! Kill the fags! Screams from a rally crowd on the cab's radio.

A reporter yells over the noise: *The anti-gay rally has reached parliament house. A handful of protesters is attempting to scale the fence.*

The driver brakes heavily for a platoon of big, yellow, Gatt Corporation graders that pull in from a side street and says over his shoulder. "Sorry about that. They're digging trenches all round Darlinghurst. New gas lines, or something."

Lana's place is across the road from Kinselas funeral parlour, just off Oxford Street at Taylor Square. I'm excited by the thought of living here. I'll be able to walk to and from work in five minutes. I'll be in the heart of things.

The cab driver pulls in behind the parlour's glass-sided funeral wagon. A thin old man, wearing a top hat, tends to the two horses topped out with black feathered headdresses.

In other news, Raft, the Australian actor and model, has been declared miss-ing. His last known whereabouts was on the set of the futuristic action thriller Trapeze being filmed at the BHP site in Newcastle. Police request anyone with information about the missing man to contact the authorities.

The cabbie kills the volume and tallies the meter. "Nine-fifty."

"Make it a tenner." I hand him the note revelling in my new ability to tip like I'm a 'somebody'. I slide out and close the door behind me.

Is the funeral wagon an omen? I try to visualise myself laid out in the middle of the wagon.

No, this isn't an omen. Our kind are spirited away in lead coffins or burnt without ceremony in case we carry the gay plague. Our bodies are not paraded solemnly through the streets.

A queasiness overcomes me as if one of the vehicle's past inhabitants has reached out with ghost fingers and groped my innards. I step back and see the pale old man watching me as he straightens the brim of his hat with practiced fingers. Straggles of thin black hair hang over his angular face.

He sweeps his hair back and fastens it beneath the hat. Something about him is familiar. "You right, lad?"

"Yeah." I crack a smile. "I'm moving in!"

He raises an eyebrow.

"Not your wagon!" I point at Belgenny, the apartment building across the road. "In there!"

We both laugh.

Lana buzzes me in with directions to the ninth floor. The metal-walled lift has none of the Burdekin lift's charm. Lana waits beyond the sliding door wrapped in a silk dressing gown. I haven't seen her in months and she's never looked so feminine. I can't remember when I stopped thinking of her as a he.

"Are you sure you haven't had the op already?"

She hugs me and I can tell she's pleased. "Where's all your blond hair gone?" she asks.

"Natural is best," I say.

"There's not a universe in existence where mouse brown is best," she exclaims, as if she's visited every one.

Her flat is one room with a kitchenette in one corner and shower and dunny in another. The walls are covered in a red flock wallpaper. A fringed lampshade hangs over the bed. She points me to the table-for-two jammed beneath the curtained windows. The radio is tuned to classical.

"What do you think?" She resumes packing the open suitcase she's laid out over the messy duvet. "Papi said I could decorate however I wanted."

"It's you to a T."

She stops folding. "I'll miss this place," she says. "The next time you'll see me I'll be Mrs Papi and living in a mansion out in the burbs."

"How can you get married?" I say. "You'll need a new birth certificate."

She shrugs. "Papi's got friends in high places."

"What's his real name?"

"If I told you I'd have to kill you, and if I do that I won't get your rent."

"Well he must be someone very powerful to pull those strings."

"I've already said too much." She shoots me a frightened look. "He'd kill me if he knew."

"Cross my heart. I haven't heard a thing."

She rounds the bed and hands me her bank details with her male name scrawled on a piece of paper.

"I'll put the rent in every fortnight," I say, as she drops into the opposite seat and lights a cigarette. Wrenching open the curtains she flicks out
the dead match. "I'm going to miss this view." She spins on her haunches
and sticks her head out the window. I follow suit. "Centrepoint Tower,
Gilligan's Island, the old sandstone gaol." She waves her cigarette at the
billboard atop Taylor Square and the giant head of a man staring down
Oxford Street advertising cologne. "I'm going to miss him the most," she
says. "That gorgeous bastard staring at me with his emerald eyes while I
drink my morning coffee."

"Raft?" I say. "He's vanished. I heard it on the radio."

"Not him too!" she says. "You've just reminded me of Donut."

"Poor Donut," I say. "None of us got to say goodbye."

"I'm going to say something now." She tosses the cigarette and, elbows
on the windowsill, steeples her fingers beneath her nose.

"Now I lay me down to sleep,
I pray the Lord my soul to keep,
If I should die before I wake,
I pray the Lord my soul to take."

"Amen," I say. "Donut would have appreciated that."

"No, he wouldn't," she says. "He would have said something awful and
bitchy, but that's why we loved him."

.5.

Pick up the tray," Nic says. "Hold it like you are taking drinks to a table."

I sit the tray on my open palm. Nic purposefully bumps it and sends it flying.

"That's no way to carry a drinks tray. There's no manoeuvrability. You must consider the tray an extension of your body."

He elevates the tray on his fingertips. "Now pretend to be a customer and bump me."

I do as he asks. Nic expertly swerves the tray around my attempt to upset him. "The next thing is drink placement," he says. "Never place the heaviest drink close to the tray's edge. You must centre it and work outwards in graduations of weight and remove them in the same order."

My training involves transporting several different sized empty bottles to the tables. The Countess sees me off from the end of the counter.

"Where are you headed?"

"Table Seven," I say.

"Bon voyage." She waves her cloth like a hanky after a disembarking ocean liner.

Table 1, I count in my head as I pass, Table 2, Table 3, Table…

The bottles tilt and fall and roll off like bombs. Glass shatters into every corner.

"Clean it up," Nic says, slicing garnish. "Try again."

*

Nic sends me upstairs to get a jar of gomme syrup. I catch the lift, walk the corridor, and push through the door that leads into the kitchen. Waiting to catch the head chef's attention I stand beside the waitress polishing cutlery.

Her hands are tomato red from plunging them into the steaming water and pulling out the silver. I smell methylated spirits. There's a new chef in the kitchen handling dough. Nice face. Boy-next-door. Dark brown hair.

The waitress catches me staring at him.

"Don't bother," she sighs. "He's straight and married."

"What a waste," I grin.

At the sound of our voices the new chef looks up.

"I'm Connor," he says. "I'd shake hands, but as you can see…"

I look at his flour and water covered hands. His wedding band peeps through the glug.

"I'm David, but everyone calls me…"

"Yes, Kit?" the head chef says before I can finish. "What is it?"

"Nic sent me up to get the gomme syrup."

"Well stop flirting with Connor." The head hands me a large container, "and get your arse back downstairs."

.6.

The Countess is called Countess for three reasons: her real name's Tess, she has a regal bearing, and she's a walking calculator. Counting customers, calculating tips, and balancing the till, adding and subtracting, doing her sums so we'll finish the shift with the maximum amount of gratuity.

She's a genius money extracting machine.

"A tip is a reward for intimacy that doesn't involve the physical," she coaches. "This relies on more than just being eagle-eyed. You must extract the customer's personal story. A polish here, a polish there, and then you feed him back his story like coins into a poker machine. Then, time to pay, one touch of his arm, voila."

"Cha-ching!" Nic says, from behind the bar.

"If I was a customer what would you say about me?" I say.

"Do you really want to know?"

"Careful, laddie," Nic warns.

"Yes. I really do."

"You carry a chip on your shoulder," she says. "Do you know what it is to carry a chip?"

I remember Ty's explanation, "It's a hurt that people carry around on their shoulders."

"Here's another version." Her voice drops an octave. "Instead of a weight that can be lifted down, or knocked off, you have an erosion." The Countess runs her finger in a sharp V from the base of my wing-tip collar down to my heart and then back to the crest of my left shoulder. "As if an axe has gouged out the flesh and bone. That's what you carry. An excision that releases a wellspring of toxic water that becomes a foaming river, and that river erodes the chip into a canyon right down to the bottom of your heart."

Her hand rests against my chest as if divining. Her voice has taken on a faraway quality.

"There's a wheelhouse on your poisoned river that's been there as long as the river itself. A pale blind animal was born there. It's your soul," she says, tapping her finger against my heart. "This creature doesn't know it, but the river is his mother, and the smacking wheelhouse is his father. With his finely tuned snout he finds the bitter grain growing along the riverbanks. The turning waterwheel drives the stone where he crushes the grain into a flour that he then mixes with the bitter water into a paste. This is his only sustenance. Do you want me to go on?"

I nod, hypnotised.

"You are bitter about what life has served you. You blame others. You need to coax that creature into the light. Lay little treats up the thin scrabble trail that scales the canyon walls and entice him."

Don't be so ridiculous, I want to say but the way they are both looking at me I sense every word she speaks is true.

"How do you do that?"

"It's a family hand-me-down," she says. "Our father has the third eye, too."

"It dodged me, thankfully," Nic says. "Our family has too many links with the other world as it is."

"Our father drives the funeral cart for Kinselas," the Countess explains.

"I know him," I say. "He parks near my building."

"Pffft," she says. "You know him? I bet you don't even look at him. He frightens people for what he represents."

"I nod when I pass."

"Next time say hello," she touches my arm. "Tell him you work with us. He'll be pleased to meet you."

"Is there anything you can't see?"

"Not much," she says, sadly. "The only thing that truly blinds is love."

*

Nic's fingers twist and turn the bowtie centimetres from my face. Occasionally his knuckles graze my chin like he's a shadow boxer. He ties my tie because I haven't yet been shown the special knot that makes the tie look like a gorgeous black bloom. "It's called the Rookwood knot," he says. A smell of cologne and nicotine wafts up from his fingers. His face in front of mine is like a father at a wedding preparing his son. He clucks my chin when he is finished. Every shift starts like this – like we're about to attend a ceremony. He grills me as he goes.

"What goes in a Golden Nail?" he growls, cigarette hanging from his mouth.

"Equal parts Scotch and Drambuie poured over ice. Large cut gold flakes. Orange twist."

"Golden Sidecar?"

"Brandy, Cointreau, lemon juice, gold cut medium."

The tying completed he pushes me to the Countess who sits at Table One with a container full of cufflinks.

The Countess is superstitious and performs a ritual at the beginning of each shift.

Her cufflink collection features etched shields, horse heads, crescent moons, automobiles, aeroplanes, dice and galleons under full sail, crocodiles, a boxer's gloves, enamel snakes, bull heads, cupids and butterflies, battleships, bicycles, and many more. Each image carries deep meaning for the Countess as she rolls the shaker back and forth.

"What do the links have in store for us tonight?" She unscrews the lid and extracts the first piece she touches.

"Top hat." She up-ends the rest and rakes her fingers through for its companion. "More money than usual will be visiting."

"More money left on the tip tray?" I say.

"Exactly."

Unhinging the toggle, she threads it through the hole in my cuff.

"What must a waiter never do?"

"Return from the floor empty-handed. Something must always be picked up or cleaned."

"What's your mantra?"

"A waiter must be an acrobat, a diplomat, and a doormat."

She nods and scrapes the pile back into the container.

"Does the same apply to a waitress?" I ask.

"Yes."

"Were you ever a doormat?"

"My sister's nobody's doormat," Nic growls. "Not anymore. She turns the bastards into *her* doormats."

The Countess hushes him.

"I am a hostess and a hostess follows different rules to those of a waitress."

At that moment Arno Gatt, scion of one of the wealthiest and most influential families in Australia comes through the door like a battering ram. Gatt cranes hang over the city pouring Gatt cement; Gatt Corporation has literally built the entire city, even Centrepoint, but one sharp look from the Countess and Arno Gatt is reduced to a lamb.

"Speak of the doormat," Nic mutters.

"Arno," the Countess scolds as she returns the container of cufflinks to its place beneath the bar. "What is the meaning of barrelling through the door like a bull in a china shop?"

"I'd like to book a table," Arno says. "Bring in father. He wants to meet you."

The Countess flicks me a look and presses the back of her hand to her forehead as if in a tragic swoon.

"Why me? To show him a doormat trodden down by life's vicissitudes? An example of how the lower-half live?"

"No! Not at all. I, I…" Arno stutters.

"Table Four," she says, penning his name into the bookings book before he can get his words out. "Six-fifteen. Be on time."

Of the 11 tables, Table One is the best and everyone knows it. No one treats a Gatt like this but Arno loves it.

"I've told Father all about you."

"You know nothing about me, Arno Gatt." She taps his watchface with the end of the pen. "Now ping-a-ling. If you arrive late you'll lose the table. Then what would your father think?"

"You're right." He turns for the door. "See you soon."

"What does vicissitudes mean?" I say, as he disappears through the door.

"Changes in fortune." She taps my cuff link as she did with Arno's watch. "Top hat means Arno's father."

"Could top hat mean death?" I say. "Your father wears one."

She turns sharply.

"Don't translate so literally, and without context. You've confused symbol with reality. Our Da worked hard his entire life. Our Da is not death. Da is represented by the scarab. I've yet to pull out his cufflink. I don't know why."

"I meant no offence," I say.

"Pffft," she says, fishing her hand into the bottle and extracting a cufflink. "You're simply ignorant. Now look at this cufflink. An Egyptian pyramid. How do you decipher this?"

"It's on the American dollar bill," I say. "So, it probably means money."

"That's it?' she says. "Just money? Use your head."

"Pharaoh, or king?"

"It also means tomb," she says.

"So that's rotten luck if you pull the pyramid?"

"Not necessarily," she says. "It's about context. A tomb can be a repository for many things. Golden crates full of treasure, sarcophagi, but how can you be sure the grave robbers haven't been? Maybe all that's left inside is memories."

.7.

The Gold Bar sits on the periphery of two worlds – the gay and the straight. It's where the conservative world mingles with the demimonde. The Golden Rule is you must have money, but Countess makes exceptions for the destitute painters and sculptors who she counts as real talent and whose drinks she puts on the bills of the rich who don't dare complain.

Countess schools the meeker artistic types: "Remember what a famous playwright once said. 'When bankers get together for dinner, they discuss art. When artists get together for dinner, they discuss money.' It's the same in a bar. Let me introduce you. You must learn to sell yourself."

"She's made more artists' careers than an early death," Nic says.

Customers come through in waves. First, the silvery minnows: the artists, designers, and curators. Then the bigger fish – doctors, advertising and film executives. Then the legal barracudas. Then the sharks from the banks. Then the killer whales – speculators and property developers – then the big blues, the mineral tycoons too huge to be brought down by anything but their own mortality and who come to guzzle gold like it's plankton.

Throughout the night the Countess moves between tables giving impromptu gold leaf readings. She deciphers the residue left in the glass like a fortune teller reads tea leaves. It's one of her many tricks. She tells me that the imagery is the same and is often more exact. Her gifts are manifold.

Nic is master and Countess is mistress and I move between them like a satellite. The Countess keeps her breath fresh with Creme de Menthe. There is always a man hanging off her every word.

*

I am wiping Table Seven, the table closest to the stairs, when a blue whale,

116

one of the biggest, one who's never visited before, appears in the doorway with his son. I check my watch: 6.15 exactly. The patrons fall silent. The face of power and money is descending into their midst.

Arno's father speaks into the silence. "A dive bar? This is where you bring me? It looks like an underground toilet."

"Father, please," Arno whispers.

The Countess moves forward to receive them. There's no way she can't have heard.

"Countess I'd like to introduce you to my father, Reiner Gatt." Arno is nervous. "Father this is the Countess."

"How do you do?" Gatt senior says. "Please call me Rhine."

"The Rhine and the Arno," the Countess allows him her hand. "Two powerful rivers in our little toilet block. I hope there'll be enough swinging room."

"I doubt it," the old man appraises her. "No doubt you've taken offence at my refence to these urine-coloured tiles."

The room is so quiet you can hear a pin drop. The Countess's laugh tinkles as she motions for them to follow her to the fourth table. "None at all. Just wash your hands once you've used the facilities. Make sure you use soap and leave a tip for those who have to clean up after your dribble."

The Rhine's surprised laugh comes out as a cough. They take their seats and I hurry over with a small dish of crudites and some water.

"My son told me you are clever," he murmurs to her. "He says you can 'read' people. I want you to 'read' me."

The Countess crosses her pale arms. "You have suffered a recent bereavement, and I am sorry for your loss, but a reading is not advisable."

"I'm the customer and it's what I want."

"Please, Countess?" Arno says.

The Countess sighs and drops her hand on the old man's shoulder. "As you wish," she says. Her eyes take on a distant quality. Several seconds tick by. A shadow flits across her face.

"You introduce yourself as the Rhine," her voice drops an octave. "The river in your heart stagnates with the corpses of your enemies. You stand on the riverbank staring down at the rotting bodies. You are looking for someone. You are never rid of the stench in your nostrils. People think the look of disdain on your face is directed outwards, but it's cast inwards. You hate what you've become but it's going to get worse because you can't stop it. You yearn for death which is why you've never taken the gold."

She strips him naked before everyone and he is momentarily helpless. The room is transfixed.

A strangled sound emanates from his throat. "Is my wife in the water?"

The Countess's eyes flick to the tip jar.

"No," she says. "She was never your enemy."

Relief softens his features and for a moment the look of disdain lifts.

"Tell me more," he says, softly.

She removes her hand from his shoulder. "I've spent more time in your heart than I care to. Now what can I get you to drink?"

With a shaking hand the old man takes a sip of his water and from the way he turns his gaze on the Countess it's obvious he's fallen under her spell. Childlike, he says, "You choose."

She retreats behind the bar and washes her hand in the sink. She whispers a directive to Nic.

What do you call this drink?" the Rhine says, admiring the two flutes of swirling golden flakes the Countess places on their folded napkins.

"It's a classic Champagne cocktail you've forced me to rename in your honour," she says. "A Golden Shower."

He laughs and takes a sip. "Delicious!"

Father and son enjoy three rounds and soon the whole bar wants Golden Showers. When it comes time to pay, the Countess tallies up the bill, folds the white paper, and writes *Thank You*. She hands it to Rhine with a slow press of his arm. On this night the Countess receives the biggest tip of her career. A thousand dollars, courtesy of the Rhine.

*

Weeks pass and the political situation outside in the broader world continues to disintegrate. Increasingly, Hygiene Army uniforms can be seen peppering the Gold Bar crowd. This new type of clientele never receives any of the Countess's air kisses and Nic underpours their drinks. They always leave quickly.

.8.

"Hey, kiddo," Nic says. "Don't forget your tray. You need to practise. Probation's nearly over."

Tray perched on fingertips I zoom up Oxford Street past the Exchange Hotel where I used to hang as a drink thieving scavenger who bled my own kind. How my vicissitudes have changed. I sidestep the wraithlike men heading for the Mirror Bar where I used to steal and wonder how I could have done that? Perhaps they'd only had enough money for one drink. Perhaps they'd come from a funeral, or from a hospital ward where they'd witnessed a friend's final gasp. I think of the pale creature the Countess said I have living in my heart. It's a jackal.

I spot Ty standing in a darkened doorway, surveying a sea of glittering glass. He holds a broom.

"What's with the tray?" he says.

"I got a job," I say. "What's with the broom?"

He ignores my question and lights a cigarette. "Where?"

"Andy Flanagan's Gold Bar."

"Where rich wankers drink gold?"

"The ancient Egyptians drank it to sustain life," I explain.

"My people have been around longer than the Egyptians and we don't eat gold."

There's no point arguing. I pull out the wad of money the Countess handed me. "Look at the tips."

Ty takes a puff on his cigarette and looks away.

"What's with the broom?"

"I got a job, too."

"Where?"

"Here." He motions to the smashed neon SAUNA sign he's pulled in off the footpath and out of the way of pedestrians.

"What happened?"

"Skinheads. They smashed up the place and beat up the patrons," He smiles grimly. "I hid in the linen closet."

"You should get a different job."

"Like yours?"

"Why not? There's plenty of bars on Oxford Street."

"When was the last time you were served by an Aboriginal man in a pub on Oxford Street?"

He watches me draw a blank.

He raises his voice over a deep motor roar, "Na, didn't think so." We turn to see a truck convoy crawling up towards us. All of Oxford Street stops to watch. I think of the skinhead centipedes. This is multiplied tenfold. This is an anaconda.

"Hygiene Army," Ty mutters. The smell of truck exhaust mingles with his cigarette and something else; the electric smell of threat.

The anaconda pulls up beside us, truck engines throbbing. Hygiene goons, their faces painted white, stare back at us through the canvas flaps.

"Shouldn't their faces be painted camouflage?" I say.

"It's that new paint that repels mozzies from landing and passing on the plague."

"We'll probably all be wearing it soon," I say.

Ty laughs. "If I paint my face white can I get a job at your joint?"

"Very funny." I change the subject. "Guess who else works for Andy?"

He shrugs.

"Johnnie. The hooker, remember? People used to call him Gloria." Something tells me to never mention to Ty that I'd slept with him.

Ty drops the cigarette and crushes it beneath the toe of his sandshoe.

"I thought he was in Brisbane," he says.

"He got out before he was thrown out."

"Is he still on the game?"

"He's Andy Flanagan's chauffeur."

"Just the chauffeur?" Ty says.

"Andy's not like that."

"Oh you fool," Ty says.

The air is thick with exhaust. Again, I'm stuck for a reply.

"Why have the trucks all stopped?"

"There's your answer," Ty says, pointing up the road to the woman weaving slowly between the vehicles. She stops and lifts one elegant gloved hand to the heavens.

"*Oooooooooooo.*"

"Trust our Goddess to stop an army," I say.

We make exaggerated bows and blow her air kisses. "Mwah! Mwah!"

A Hygiene soldier watching from the closest truck leans out, lifts two fingers, cocks his thumb, and shoots. His invisible bullet hits my heart and ricochets around my vitals. I see with terrible clarity just how vulnerable Ty and I are to the vicissitudes of the world around us. Ty is enjoying himself bowing and scraping to the Opera Lady so I keep the wound to myself.

.9.

The day of reckoning arrives. Nic assembles three cocktails. A daiquiri, a salt encrusted margarita, and a gold martini.

"Olive or twist?" Nic says.

"Twist," I say. "For Lady Luck."

"You don't need luck," Nic says.

"Never say that!" the Countess hisses. She picks up a pinch of salt from the salting saucer and tosses it over her left shoulder. "Luck is the secret ingredient!"

I centre the drinks outwards in graduations of weight and prepare to lift the load.

"Here goes." I hoist the tray to shoulder level.

"We'll meet again…" The Countess waves her cloth sadly. "Don't know where. Don't know when… But I know we'll meet again some sunny day."

I am the drink server. This is what I do. This is what I've always done. I deliver the perfect drink. From elbow to wrist my arm is the powerful stalk that holds up Centrepoint. My arm can withstand earthquakes and wind gusts of cyclonic strength. If my tendons were laid out, they would stretch to New Zealand. I know how many steps I must take before every landing. My shoes know each step, each carpet impression.

On the first floor landing I see Nic and the Countess slide by in the lift as they ascend to hear the outcome. The Countess is still singing.

On the second floor landing a section of salt crusting the glass rim of the margarita falls to the napkinned surface of the tray. I almost falter. Does fallen salt granules from the glass rim constitute a drink drop? Will I be disqualified? Must I go back to stealing drinks and scabbing money?

I ascend the final flight and step onto the parquetry landing. Andy Flanagan and three restaurant waitresses – the judging panel – stand behind a table set up to receive the drinks tray. The Countess and Nic wait by the lift door looking cautiously optimistic. The skylight glows overhead and I can hear the coo of pigeons on the roof and a distant helicopter. I lower the tray safely and step back.

The judges gather round the tray in a whispering circle. Their decision must be unanimous.

Between thumb and forefinger Andy Flanagan picks up the fallen salt and holds the granules up to the skylight.

"There has been droppage," he declares.

I'm doomed.

"That's my fault," Nic complains. "I made the crust too thick."

"Shush," the Countess says.

"But droppage is not spillage." Andy Flanagan flings the grains over his left shoulder. "After careful consideration it has been decided that you have passed probation. You are, forthwith, a permanent employee of this establishment."

Andy Flanagan launches forward and pumps my hand as clapping and whooping erupts from all around. The sound bounces off the restaurant door and flies into the skylight where it rains back down like someone is even cheering on the roof.

Nic pulls me into a quick tight hug and the Countess grips my arm.

*

Nic takes me to be fitted for my tuxedo jacket and trousers at Zink & Sons, my new threads are put on Andy Flanagan's tab to be paid off incrementally. Zink outfits everyone in the city. They're the 'go to' for any man needing a suit, from cemetery attendants to the wealthiest CEO. I am now among their ranks.

As the tailor runs his measuring tape along my arm I gaze back along its length and out across the street to my old begging corner.

Being outfitted for my first suit should be a celebration but all I can see is the Pied Piper telling me I must be a real boy and now here I am being turned into one.

*

The first drink Nic teaches me to make is the non-alcoholic Citron Pressé.

Fill a highball glass with ice to the brim. Pour a thumbnail's depth of lemon juice over the ice, then a dash of gomme syrup. Garnish with the thinnest slice of lemon. Insert a straw for stirring. Place a folded napkin on the table before the customer. Then place a small jug of still water beside the highball. The customer does the rest.

*

After work Nic and I go drinking at the Exchange to celebrate my being made permanent. We sit side-by-side at the front bar. Nic is a well-known face and I'm his little sidekick. Without my bleached hair and other artificial add-ons, I'm unrecognisable as the drink stealing scab. Now I'm just another waiter with tips to blow.

A barman sets a line of drinks on fire amid customers' 'oohhs and aahhs'.

"Flaming Lamborghinis," Nic mutters. "Stupid drink. Why burn alcohol?"

A young woman rushes into the bar handing out flyers. She thrusts one at me.

Fuck the Emergency State

Over 50 people have been detained, three have been killed. The Hygiene Army has been given complete power to arrest, search, detain and interrogate. This State of Emergency is a torturer's charter. Join the picket outside Government House. This Thursday 4pm.

"What do you think's going to happen with the Hygiene Army?" I ask Nic, as he lights a cigarette.

"Hatred is a cocktail," he says, blowing smoke. "A jigger of paranoia, fear, and disgust. Garnished with envy and set on fire like that stupid drink. It'll flare and soon be over."

.10.

"Census! Compulsory. Open up!" All morning, hard knocking and gruff voices calling throughout the Belgenny apartment building.

Two males at my door. One a ferret, the other a warthog. "How many occupants? Male? Female? Married? Single? Gay, Straight, Bisexual? Occupation. Last time you were sick? Any sores? Smoker/non-smoker? Ongoing cough? Do you take recreational drugs?" Sniffing round. Looking over my shoulder. Same questions. It's laughable if the government thinks anyone would tell these bozos the truth.

I hear people lying about themselves all up and down my corridor.

I butch it up. Or try to.

"Male. Heterosexual. The little lady's away. She's a make-up artiste. I'm a cocktail barman up the Cross. Orgasms. Sex on the Beach. Slippery nipples, that sorta thing. No illnesses. Ex-smoker, or at least tryin'. It's hard ya know? No sores. Whaddaya mean? Like blisters? Acne? Nuffin. No drugs. Wat are ya? A copper?"

*

Violence. A waiter from a big city hotel is murdered in Hyde Park as he walks home from his night shift. His body is found floating in the fountain at the base of the minotaur's plinth. His name was Shane, or Shawna.

Nic teaches me how to clench my wine knife with the corkscrew between my middle and ring finger and the blade extended out past my base of my little finger like a platypus spur. He teaches me a punching, turning, weaving dance with it and tells me to aim for the jugular. It's like having my box-cutter again.

The Dykes on Bikes organise themselves to protect the denizens of the street by roaring up and down trying to keep an eye on everything, but they're spread thin. Cops are non-existent and there are rumours they're cruising around in unmarked cars in plainclothes doing half the bashing.

.11.

Bill & Toni's on Stanley Street do 'all day' breakfasts. It's the hangout for all the waiters, concierges, DJs, and barmen who keep the night-time city alive. Music plays softly while Ty, Johnnie and I read the papers over bacon and eggs, and black coffee.

Ty stabs the front page of the *Sydney Morning Herald* with his fork. "It says here that doctors must notify the Department of Health and Hygiene of all their homosexual patients. They don't even need proof, just a suspicion."

"A doctor felt me up once," Johnnie laughs. "So he's stuck somewhere between a rock and a hard place."

"Do you mind?" I say. "I haven't finished eating."

Johnnie grins and turns his page of the *Star Observer*. He blanches at all the faces of the dead framed in black. "Fuck, I used to work with this guy."

"Show me," Ty takes the paper.

"See you on the dancefloor in heaven," Ty says, reading the obit attached to the photo. "Love from the boys at Bennies? I didn't know you worked for the Pied Piper?"

"I didn't," Johnnie stammers. "It was another place a long time ago."

"Sure," Ty sighs.

"There's poor Shawna," Johnnie changes the subject, pointing at the black inked lined photo of the waiter smiling at a work Christmas party. His co-workers also placed the obituary. There's no mention of his family.

"Their ghosts are all lined up waiting for the Opera Lady," I say.

"What are you on about?" Ty says.

"This bloke I once knew said the Opera Lady was a medium between this world and the next and that when she sang the ghosts would lift off and fly to heaven."

"I hope it's true." Johnnie slurps his coffee.

Turning a page, I come face-to-face with a full-page advertisement for the Hygiene Army. **Become Hygienic Now!** A uniformed blond boy stands saluting. It's Bondi. Behind him in rows, a phalanx of uniformed young men and women.

"Jesus," I say, twisting the page for the others. "This is the nutjob that tried to kill us at South Bondi."

"Looks like the nutjob found the perfect nut job," Ty says.

"The whole world's crazy," Johnnie says. "We gotta keep our heads down."

"I told the census idiots I was straight and married," I laugh.

"God if they believed that they'd believe anything," Ty says.

"What did you tell them?" I challenge.

"That I'm a faggot who likes romantic walks on the beach drinking Pina Coladas."

"Midnight walks will get you killed down Bondi way," I say. "And I wouldn't be seen dead drinking a Pina Colada."

"That's because you're a snob now you work at the Gold Bar."

"You're just jealous."

"Cease fire," Johnnie says, waving his hand between us. "Life's too short."

"Life's too fucking short for bullshit and lies!" Ty downs his coffee and pushes back his chair. He peels a 20 from a roll in his pocket and tosses it on the table. "Can't either of you two idiots see what's happening out there in the world? Don't either of you ever think about politics?"

"Nup," I goad him. "Ignorance is bliss."

Ty stalks off. Johnnie calls after him, "Oh Ty, don't get the shits."

"Let him go," I say. "He'll cool down."

"The census didn't come to the garage," Johnnie says at the till as we're paying. "So I guess they don't know I live there."

"The less the government knows the better," I say.

*

After breakfast I walk to the Boy Charlton Pool thinking about what Ty said about politics. Thinking about how the world hates us. That powerful message of hate that permeates the air I'm breathing. I tell myself, who'd want to think about that? I want to ignore it because I'm afraid I'll start to believe it again like I did when I was a kid. I'm scared my mind's not strong enough to build defences. I shouldn't have to build defences. I should just be able to live my life. As I said: ignorance is bliss. Less blissful now I've fought with Ty. Am I a snob? What's a snob? Someone who thinks he's better than anybody else. No, I'm not a snob. I just feel lucky I've got a job that tips.

At the pool I remove my clothes in the changeroom and pull on my togs. I swim a kilometre each day to help shift the smoke from my lungs. As I cross the compound the soft, slap, slap, slap, of the Aussie crawlers is over-taken by the raucous screeching of cockatoos in the Botanic Gardens and jackhammering from the naval base.

All the Oxford Street beauties are arranged on towels at the deep end, the hottest ones are lying closest to the dive blocks. Janis, Cha Cha, and Cora, from the Albury, Karen from the Oxford, and Urshula from the Exchange. They're the top shelf queens – the ones so hot their looks aren't diminished by their silly girls' names. The hotter the queen the sillier the name. That's how it goes. I guess it's so they don't get so full of themselves they disap-pear up their own perfect arses. None of us would care though – we'd all happily follow them.

I lay my towel among the B-crowd; the less attractive barmen and wait-ers, chefs and kitchen staff. I might earn the most in tips but that's not the currency used here. Here it's all about looks and the B-crowd is where I belong. And then there are the exotic blow-ins. Flight stewards from inter-national airlines on stopovers in the city. Birds with no names who will return home with breathless stories of the beauties of Sydney.

The spot where Shawna used to spread his towel lies empty except for a small handful of yellow flowers someone's laid in his honour.

Apart from the squawk of the American flight stewards flown Down Under, talk between the locals is subdued. The weight of what has happened to one of our own lies heavy.

I amble to the diving blocks trying not to look self-conscious. I swing each foot in front of me like I'm wearing flippers, like Quoll's father told him to do, a handy visual aid to walk like a man. Centrepoint Tower glows like a golden trophy just out of reach as I step up on my launchpad and fix my goggles. I dive and zoom along the bottom through the sunlight spears.

I'm a fast swimmer. After a lap to find my rhythm, I plough 19 more, rolling like a seal at each end to push off, before I climb the silver ladder and sun myself standing against the hot grey cement wall. This is when I look best, but I must remember Quoll relating his father's dictate, 'stand with your legs apart, not with your legs together. You're not a woman with something to protect.' It feels like a betrayal to Quoll, taking on his father's orders – but I can't help it.

Men from the B crowd lie on their towels gazing over the rims of their Ray-Bans. Posing and acting casual they turn lazily to scratch a calf muscle or buttock while I, just as casually, pretend to gaze across Woolloomooloo Bay to the navy ships or focus on the Kings Cross skyline.

I gather up my things and head for the showers. One of the American flight stewards, a swarthy one, follows and stands in the opposite cubicle. He's glancing over, so I remove my togs and give him a full-frontal view. He invites me back to his hotel where the airline stables its crews.

He insists I wear two condoms, one rolled down over the other. From the look in his eyes it's not to protect me.

"Where do you think I've been?" I say, trying to sound light-hearted.

I should tell him to do the same, because he's American, but two's overkill.

.12.

The young man who dreamt up the Grim Reaper advert sits at Table Three coasting on the wave of success created by his images of death and terror. He has long, combed, golden hair like a '70s surfer girl.

I must place his Golden Goose cocktail before him and smile benignly. Ensure his ashtray is clean. No more than three butts is the rule. An unintended consequence of the advert's success, he's the reason Oxford Street is awash with thugs. He's the reason I have to weave, duck, and run. I want to pour his drink over him and upend the ashtray in his lap, but I am a professional doormat. That's my role. A good waiter is a doormat, an acrobat, and a diplomat, and this is my lot.

A group of uniformed soldiers come into the bar. Bondi is among them. "It's table service," the Countess says. "Come and sit."

She leads them to Table 11. Siberia.

Bondi looks about. His eyes graze across my face but he fails to recognise me from the stone throwing incident. For the first time in my life I'm pleased I look like nothing. The Countess serves them, and they leave after one expensive, weak drink.

Gatt senior begins to date again. He appears at the head of the stairs with Isadora, the favoured seamstress of his dead wife. Arno tells the Countess he's unbothered about his father's new paramour, but it's clear from the wounded look in his eyes he's hurt his mother has been replaced so quickly.

*

After the restaurant closes for the night, chefs, waiters, and waitresses, descend for staff drinks. It's on them I practise drink-making. Staff are allowed the bottom shelf house spirits only. Second and top shelf are off limits, so is the gold.

"How do I measure without drink servers?" I ask Nic.

"Free-pouring is done by counting." Nic demonstrates by pouring vodka into a cocktail mixer. "1-2-3-4."

Dark alcohol like scotch, bourbon, and dark rum, is poured in a squat tumbler style glass called an old-fashioned. Clear alcohol – gin, vodka, tequila – is served in highballs. Men drink from the old-fashioned, and women from highballs. There are exceptions but that's the general rule.

The new chef Connor and I form an agreement. He'll hide crème caramels behind the produce boxes in the storeroom for me when I ascend to pick up the gomme syrup, on the proviso I make his staff drinks extra strong.

For Connor's drink I count to six. I know he's married, but I'm a bit in love with him. He has that dependable boy-next-door look, and thick brown hair that falls in a slab across his hazel eyes.

I'm standing in the 3rd floor storeroom gorging crème caramel when Connor enters to pick up some flour. Through the window Centrepoint is lit up and magnificent.

"It's like a golden toffee apple stuck in the heart of the city," I say.

"It's like a syringe," he says.

*

After work, Johnnie, Ty, and I, meet up at the Exchange Hotel.

"I made 80 bucks in tips tonight," Rusty, the waiter from The Paddington Hotel brags. The others look impressed until I say, "I made $120." It's official. I'm the richest drinks waiter in town.

The Pied Piper enters with his stable of boys, including the tall blond twins. They slap their fat wallets down on the next table. In tight, white tees, and distressed denims, the Piper's boys look like Bruce Weber models posing as belligerent grease monkeys. From the looks of their wallets any one of them has more money than all us drink waiters combined. Bambino, sans red beanie, stands among them. His cheeks are hollow which makes him look the most sooky. His eyes slide past mine without acknowledgment.

"Well, well, well, if it ain't Johnnie," The Pied Piper says, throwing his voice at our table. "How's tricks, Poker Chip? Oh, that's right, you're a glorified taxi driver now. Come back to us when you're bored."

The garage attendants laugh like he's said the funniest thing in the world.

Johnnie turns red. "I'm happy being a chauffeur."

"Well how the mighty have fallen," the Pied Piper says, in pretend astonishment. "You know where we are when you change your mind."

"I won't be changing my mind," Johnnie says.

"Don't bet on it," the Pied Piper says, slyly before turning away.

"Let's go find another bar," Johnnie says, draining his drink. "This place stinks."

"Na, you go," Ty says, tartly. "I'm staying put."

"Why?" Johnnie says.

"I prefer the stink of truth to the stink of lies," Ty says.

"Suit yourself." Johnnie heads for the door.

I'm confused by what just happened between them but, from the thunderous look on Ty's face, as he heads to the bar, think it's best not to ask.

Ty returns with two drinks and a packet of tomato flavoured potato chips. He breaks the bag open and sits it in the middle of the table.

"Mind if I have one?" I say.

"Go right ahead."

I lift a chip from the pack. "Remember your theory about people with chips on their shoulders?" I say. "From back when we used to hang at the football ground?"

"I remember," he says. "It was dreamt up by that government-appointed shrink I saw back in the children's home."

"You said the worst chip was the tomato chip. You said it was the colour of blood and violence."

"Yeah, well right now I reckon it's the best," he says.

I'm drunk. Ty's left, and I'm on my own. 'Undecided' by Plan 8 is screeching out of the speaker boxes.

I position myself beside Bambino at the bar. "Do you remember me?" I say.

"Should I?" he says, looking like a poster of Jimmy Dean in *Rebel Without a Cause*.

"I gave you my box-cutter and a handful of money when you first got off the bus."

"You look completely different," he says.

"You too."

"It didn't take long to get acclimatised," he says.

"Remember, I left you sitting on the step out front?" I'm unable to disguise the reproach. "I came back and you were gone."

He stubs his cigarette into the ashtray. "My benefactor came along."

"You thought the Pied Piper was your benefactor?" I say, horrified.

"When he said his name was Bennie, I heard 'bene-factor'." He swills back a mouthful of drink. "Easy mistake. Truth is, I didn't even know what a 'benefactor' was."

"He was a guy called Quoll," I say. "He saw you first when you got down off the bus."

"Too late now," he says.

"Yeah," I say. "He died not long after."

"So, are you still a scab?"

I guess he isn't going to offer any condolences.

"I work in a cocktail bar."

"Ha! Sounds like my job," he smirks. "Can you give me an Orgasm?"

"Don't be tacky."

"Sorry. Bennie the Boss likes me to talk a certain way." His hand performs a wave motion. "Cut to the chase to make time for the next client, and the next, and the next."

I suddenly see myself plucking the $20 note off his mother and revealing her son was lost to a brothel. That's the true definition of 'tacky'. I figure it's too late to tell him she'd come looking.

"I should be the one saying sorry," I say. "I just wish I'd said 'secret admirer' instead of 'benefactor.'"

"No sweat," he says. "I should have studied more at school. You know, I still carry that knife of yours in my boot. It's saved me a few times, so I reckon I owe ya."

"You don't owe me anything."

"Listen," he says, dropping his voice. "You got a place? I need to get away from Bennie and the boys. You couldn't help me before, so help me now."

"Why do you have to get away from the Pied Piper?"

"I found out something about him and his French mate."

I take him back to Lana's. We strip down to our undies and crawl under the duvet.

He's shivering and I wrap my arms around him. "What did you find out?"

"A boy died and they dumped his body."

He tells me he can't cum because he has to save it for his clients. Clients like to see a result. So do lovers, but unless I'm going to pay him, the client wins. I close my heart off.

The next morning I wake to find him gone.

.13.

A dinner reservation. As soon as they enter, I recognise Quoll's parents. His father is wearing a Hygiene Party button pinned to his lapel like a war medal. I lead them up the red carpeted stairs to the ground floor lift, open the black grill and usher them in. They stand silently behind me as I pull the doors closed and push the bakelite button. I slip my hand in my pocket and feel Quoll turning over in his grave.

"Are you here for a special occasion?" I turn to register their faces. "A child's birthday or achievement?"

"We have no children," the man says gruffly.

"No," the woman looks down to hide the pain in her eyes and adjusts the fur about her shoulders. "We've been meaning to eat here for ages."

I hear Quoll whisper me directions.

"Well, your timing is perfect," I tell her. "As you are our 500th customer, you each win a special black daiquiri."

"Oh, my," she says to her husband. "Aren't we lucky!"

I accompany the couple to their table, pour them their water, and tell them I'll be straight back with their drinks.

The stairs are much quicker than the lift. I fly down them three at a time, pull out $50 of my own money and hand it to the Countess, "That couple ordered two black daiquiris and said keep the change."

Nic prepares the drink in the blender. Ice, dark and white rum, Cointreau, two scoops of blackberries, lemon juice, sugar syrup, and bitters. He pours the dense black soup into tall glasses, inserts long straws, and drapes the frozen fluid with a simple garnish of a gold spiral.

"Perfection," I say.

"Take them before they melt," he answers.

I stop on the second landing. I am as poised as Centrepoint Tower. Nothing will upset me. One-handed, I extract the cigarette case from my pocket, open it carefully, and sprinkle Quoll dust evenly between his parents. I use the straws to stir him through.

"Goodbye dear friend," I murmur, as he disappears into the purple black ice.

"I'm looking forward to this," the woman says, as I place the drinks before them.

I watch as they take their first sips and leave them to peruse their menus.

"How was your drink?" I ask, later as they leave through the bar.

She smiled and said dreamily, "Lovely. We drank it all." Her husband said, "I thought mine was a bit gritty."

I nodded. "That would have been seed."

.14.

Blood gushes from Nic's finger. A shard of glass glistens red on the floor.

I rush with a bar cloth to staunch the wound.

"Get the fuck away!" He snatches up the first aid kit and retreats to the cellar.

"Is it bad?" The Countess returns from attending a customer's needs.

Nic's only ever shown me patience and kindness. Hurt by his tone I can only nod.

The Countess checks on Nic, dials Andy and relays what's happened. Returning the phone to the receiver, she says, "Johnnie is bringing the car around and Andy will take Nic to Dr Edelsten's. I'll do the floor and you must make the drinks. Time to shine," she adds, kindly.

I one-two-three-four like Nic. Grind gold like Nic. Light cigarettes like Nic, wipe down the bar and keep everything moving like Nic. But I know I'm a poor estimation.

When he returns with his hand heavily bandaged I sense him watching me, gauging my moves.

He approaches at shift's end after all the customers have gone.

"You did well," he says quietly. "I'm proud of you."

"We're all proud of you," the Countess says over the haul she is counting from the upended tip jar.

"I'm sorry I yelled," Nic says. "I shouldn't have, but I had to make sure you were safe."

"I understand."

"Do you know why I yelled?"

"You've got the disease," I say flatly.

"Yes," he says, "but don't be afraid. You're more a danger to me than I am to you. If you are ill stay away. If I catch something even minor like a cold it could kill me."

140

.15.

It's 10pm, the busiest time, when Connor and his wife, Milly, come through from the Dining Room upstairs. The two have linked hands and Milly is in the lead. I'm standing behind the counter when they forge into the grey heaving sea of moneymen and lawyers.

Connor's hair is still glossy but his cheeks have slightly hollowed. I haven't seen him for a month. And now here he is, headed for the exit, having brought his wife in to show her where he'd worked. I miss him, and I miss my crème caramels.

Drink? I mouth, hoisting up an empty glass. It's all I can think to do.

He smiles a crooked smile, shakes his head, and continues at a dog paddle pace through the crowd.

No one knew why he'd stopped working, or what ailed him. No one guessed. Not at first anyway. Then came the whispers. I couldn't believe it. Not Connor. Then came the theories. First, he'd had a minor surgical procedure in Asia. Next he'd shared a needle when he'd been the drummer in a high school band. Everyone else I know got it from straightforward fucking. No questions asked. Not Connor. Connor is the curiosity and the anomaly. He's the sweet married man being fucked by the gay disease. Hence his decision to stop working.

When Connor reaches the top of the stairs that led to the street he turns and looks back over the crowd. Customers are crying out for drinks – six deep at the bar – and I can't stop to wave goodbye.

.16.

I'm drunk. Standing beside two pretty boys at the front bar of the Exchange Hotel waiting to be served, I try not to look too under the influence.

"Slit his own throat with that box-cutter he always carried," the less pretty of the two says over the music to his companion. "Selfish bastard. Bennie made me clean it up."

Their words slice open my drunken fog. Maybe I'm mistaken. Maybe they're talking about someone else. But box-cutter? Bennie?

I lean into their space. "Do you work for the Pied Piper?"

"We're clocked off," the prettier one says rudely like I'm a john.

"Are you talking about Nathan?" I say, using his real name.

"What's it to ya?" he says.

"I know him."

"He's clocked off too, gone to heaven or hell, whichever you prefer. Now fuck off out of our conversation."

I can only gasp. My box-cutter did that slicing. The one I stole back in Brisbane opening biscuit cartons and stacking shelves. The one I handed him to protect himself.

I stumble from the bar and out onto Oxford Street.

Human shapes hurry by and cars roar past. My tears make the traffic lights glitter into four times their actual size and I can't see what's coming.

"Did the fairy get it's heart broken?" a voice snarls.

I wipe my eyes with the back of my hand. Three goons outside Zink & Sons.

My face is slammed into the glass frontage. Blood spurts from my nose. An abyss opens before me. I begin to fall.

"You didn't answer my question." A fist buries itself in my stomach. I double over in agony and vomit flies over the bitumen. The goons step back. "Filthy fuck!" one of them hisses. I watch my blood drop like grenadine into the yellow vomit puddle.

I'm about to pass out when Nic's voice echoes in my mind bringing me back to myself. You must be smarter than them!

Yes.

I smear my hands against my nostrils and raise bloodied claws. I flick the droplets from my fingers and rasp, "Get the fuck away! One scratch and you're dead!"

Fear in their eyes. The violence evaporates. They turn tail and run.

*

That same night Johnnie is beaten on Crown Street walking back from buying cigarettes. Who knows? Maybe even by the same guys who got me. He's in St Vincents for a week and a half.

.17.

"There ya go," Ty jumps down from the chair beside Johnnie's bed in the mezzanine above where Andy Flanagan garages his car.

"I love it." Johnnie, speaking slowly, gazes up at the circular webbed construction that Ty has pinned to the garage ceiling. "What's it called?"

"A dreamcatcher," Ty says. "The hippie at the Oxford Square market said it's American Indian. It catches bad dreams and only lets you have good ones. It'll help you heal quicker."

"By this afternoon?" Johnnie slurs through broken teeth.

"Your leg's in a cast, you've got busted ribs, and two black eyes," I say. "I don't like your chances. Have you got a hot date?"

"Andy Flanagan hosts a card game the last Sunday of every month and I'm his Boy Sunday."

"What's a Boy Sunday?"

"Like Boy Friday to Robinson Crusoe," Ty says casually, from where he's taken a perch on the windowsill. "Like Tonto to the Lone Ranger. His slave in other words."

"Ignore him." Johnnie squints at me. "Could you do it?"

"What?"

"Let the guests in. Take jackets, refresh beers, make sure there's enough nibbles."

"Is the game on the fourth floor? I'd love to get a gander at his apartment."

"No, down in the bar."

"Have you been up there?" I say.

"They always come downstairs and meet me here in the garage."

"Who's they?" I say, confused.

"Did I say they?" he colours. "I meant him."

"Hello?" a voice calls from below. "Can I come up?"

Ty leans out over the bannister.

"Here's the Lone Ranger now," he says.

Footsteps ascend. Andy Flanagan appears wearing a pale-blue linen suit. Holding a pot-plant covered in little purple flowers, he looks like a 1930s black-and-white film star come to visit in colour.

"How's the patient?" he says looking around. He gives me a friendly nod then sees Ty by the window. He extends his hand disturbing the dust motes in the bar of sunlight. "You must be Ty. Johnnie's told me so much about you."

Ty gives a curt nod but doesn't take it. "I've heard about you, too."

Andy drops his hand and turns to Johnnie. "This African violet is a get well present. Don't get water on the leaves. It makes them rot."

"Thanks boss," Johnnie says thickly through his injuries. "I've got something for you too. I found you a Boy Sunday."

"I'm sure I can manage for one game." Andy places the plant beneath a lamp on the side table.

"Please let him," Johnnie says. "I won't feel so bad."

"I'm not doing anything else," I say.

Andy turns to me, "But isn't this your day off?"

"I'm here already," I say. "I may as well stay."

"I suppose, if it makes Johnnie happy," Andy says.

Silence falls. The awkwardness left by Ty's refusal to shake Andy's hand lingers in the air.

Andy looks around. "Who knew this loft area could be made so pleasant," he says.

"It's the best home I've ever had," Johnnie says.

"That's wonderful to hear!" Andy says. "I better go and leave you all to catch up."

Johnnie waves the felt pen. "Sign my cast?"

"Sure." Andy reads out the two messages already there. "Ty wuz here and wasn't impressed, and Snap! by Kit."

He bends down and writes *Ut tam cito*, followed by his initials, *A.F.*

"What's that mean?" Johnnie says.

145

"Latin for get well soon."

Andy looks at me. "I'll see you this afternoon."

"God, even his graffiti is pretentious," Ty says while Andy's footfalls can still be heard on the stairs.

"What's your problem?" Johnnie says, after the external door has closed. "Why didn't you shake his hand?"

"And risk being wrapped round his little finger like you two morons?" Ty says, crossing his arms. "No fucking way! I'm not gonna be his Boy Wednesday!"

"For fuck's sake," Johnnie says. "You clean the loos in a gay sauna. How's that better than working for Andy Flanagan?"

Ty's jaw is rigid.

"You wanna know why?" he says. "Because nobody owns me! The Pied Piper called you 'Poker Chip'. He also said 'you could come back'. You told us you'd never worked for him."

"I worked for him for a split second when I moved down from Brisbane," Johnnie says. "It wasn't worth mentioning."

"And the fact he called you Poker Chip?" Ty says, leaning forward like an egret about to stab a fish, "has that got anything to do with this card game you're a slave at?"

"So what if the Pied Piper is there?" Johnnie says angrily.

"The Pied Piper will be at this game?" I say, with disbelief. "Why would Andy want to hang out with the Pied Piper?"

"Not so snow white now, is he?" Ty gloats.

"Leave Andy out of it. He's one of the good guys," Johnnie says.

"Oh, it suddenly makes sense!" Ty exclaims. "Flanagan won you in a poker game, didn't he? That's why the Pied Piper called you Poker Chip. That's how you got this job!"

"No!" Johnnie looks stricken.

"Just stop with the lies," Ty spits. "I'm fucken' out of here." He thumps down the stairs and slams the door.

"Were you really won in a card game?" I say.

He nods. "You were too."

"Don't be daft," I say. "I had an interview."

"That was all staged," Johnnie says. "He won you off the French banker."

"But why? He hasn't touched me."

"He hasn't touched me either," Johnnie says. "Andy rescues people."

"Why?"

"To put us on a better path."

"But what about the tray-carrying test?"

"That was all true, but if you failed he would have found you a different job."

I don't know how to feel. A part of me feels like I should be disgusted but I'm actually sort of flattered. It makes me feel that I'm worth something. But one thing doesn't make sense.

"What stops me from leaving and doing what I want?"

"Nothing," Johnnie says. "It's an opportunity that's all. It's up to you to recognise it."

I get up. "I need to find Ty. Try to calm him down."

"Yes," Johnnie says.

"I'm not going to tell him."

"No. Better not."

I find Ty back at the small outdoor market at Oxford Square where we bought the dream catcher. "What was all that about?"

"There's shit you don't know," Ty says, wandering between the stalls.

"More shit?" I say. "How much shit is there?"

"Tons," he says. "This town is covered in it."

Ty stops at a stall selling odd bits of electrical equipment and picks up a little kid's pirate-ship night light.

"Johnnie and I grew up in the same orphanage." He turns the ship over and reveals a nasty burn. He tosses the light back on the pile and picks up an alarm clock. He gives it a shake.

"That's five dollars," the bloke behind the stall says. "If you break it ya buy it."

Ty shrugs and puts it back down. "It's busted already."

He runs his hand over a mint-green '50s Mixmaster. "The people who ran the orphanage caught us mucking around. We were just kids clinging together. They kept screaming at us 'only married people do that!' They screamed a whole lot more but that's the bit I remember."

"How much is this?" he says to the stall holder.

"35."

"Ouch," Ty says.

It's the stall holder's time to shrug. "It's retro."

"The last thing we did before they moved him to another facility was stage a little wedding with all the other kids as witnesses. The next time I saw him was a year-and-a-half later at the Terminus. We got together again but broke up because of what he did for work. I guess I always took our vows seriously."

"Why have you never told me this?"

"I wanted to forget."

"He was your first love. You can't forget."

He looks me dead in the eye.

"Wanna bet?"

.18.

Andy presents me with a list of five names of who to expect.

The Governor is the first to arrive. He unfolds himself from his government staff car with a crisp, "How do you do?"

Next is the Redhead – named, Andy informed me, not because of her hair colour but after the brand of matches she uses to burn down her own buildings to claim the insurance.

The third is Saki, the construction company competitor to the Gatts, and the only hetero on the list.

Fourth is the French banker.

"Well, if it isn't my old paramour?" he says, exiting the cab. "How are you finding working for Mr Flanagan? Does he treat you well?"

"Very," I say.

"As well as me?" He smirks, standing close.

In my head I hear Nic's voice telling me to be a diplomat.

"It doesn't involve extracurricular activities, if that's what you mean."

"Oh," he says, squeezing my groin. "You must miss this."

"Not really." I nudge his hand away.

"A little slut like you?" he whispers. "I can't believe it!"

He steps through the door and turns with a sly look. "I suspect you know the circumstances of your employment, yes? You're no more than a silly toy won at a carnival? Like a doll on a stick."

I think hard: "Better Andy's doll, than your Dagwood Dog."

"Bravo!" he pouts, tipping his head to the side. "But be careful. Sticks break and dolls drop off into the mud where no one will pick them up ever again."

All I can do is give him the last word. Nic would be proud.

The last to arrive is the Pied Piper. He looks me up and down like he's never seen me before. He deigns to speak. "Where's Poker Chip?"

"He's indisposed," I say, following him in and drawing the bolt.

The game commences. I quickly abandon any hope of understanding or following the rules, except that instead of money, they play for paintings, sculptures and other valuables objects. As the games progress, I use the time to dismantle and polish the bar and, in between, I replenish their drinks and clean out their ashtrays.

The game develops to the point where Andy Flanagan and the Pied Piper are the last two playing.

"What's at stake?" Andy Flanagan says.

"Your car and driver," the Piper says.

"You can play for the vehicle," Andy Flanagan says, "but not for Johnnie."

"Sorry bud," the Piper says. "That's the rules."

"We only have three," the Governor ticks his fingers. "Number one: all winnings are to be handed over as quickly as possible. Two: once the game has started there's no leaving the table, or else you'll forfeit. Three: nothing's off the table if it's been on the table."

"And Poker Chip's been on the table," the Pied Piper gestures obscenely, "and under it."

"Must you?" Red Head says. "Andy, what are you playing for?"

"An amendment," he says. "So this game will stop repeating itself, ad nauseum. That if I win this game…" he glances sideways at me, "none of my staff will ever be on this table again."

"Flanagan don't be so coy," Frenchie says. "My obsolete paramour over there knows you won him in a game. We discussed it at the front door."

I give Andy the thumbs up. "We can talk about it later," he tells me.

The Piper rubs his hands. "So after I've won Poker Chip back you can never play for him again? Deal!"

"Or Kit. Or Nic," Andy says.

Nic was won in a game? I think. From which of these freaks?

"I don't want either of them," the Piper says.

Why not? You used to. Am I too old?

The game begins. All eyes follow the cards. I'm not religious but I say a prayer for Johnnie.

A man appears standing swaying in the internal doorway wearing pyjama pants and a dressing gown covered in a striking geometric pattern. His thick black hair hangs low over his face. He has a crumpled look as if he has just woken, but his eyes are unseeing. He steps barefoot onto the tiles and shuffles towards the front door. The belt of his dressing gown slides undone, and his gown opens like theatre curtains revealing a ribcage spotted with purple lesions.

"Is *that* Raft?" Frenchie says.

Andy Flanagan swivels in his seat.

I hear Lana's voice in my head: cleft chin, eyes for sin.

"He's sleepwalking," Andy whispers.

"He's sick," Red says.

"You crafty dog," Saki says. "You've been hiding him here this whole time?"

"He lives here," Andy says, rising from the table. "I haven't been hiding anyone."

"Andy, remember the rules," the Governor warns. "If you leave the table you'll have to forfeit."

The Pied Piper throws up his hands. "Why'd ya have to open ya big gob?"

The Governor shrugs.

"He needs my help," Andy says. "It's his medication."

"Rules are rules," Frenchie leans back enjoying the show.

The Pied Piper indicates me. "Get your boy to shake him awake."

Raft begins to fumble with the front door lock. "Never wake a sleepwalker!" Red says. "The shock can kill. You've got to guide him back to bed."

I step from behind the bar. "I'll do it."

"Yes, that's right!" Frenchie gloats. "Earn your keep, boy!"

Andy searches through his jacket pockets, hissing, "Keep your voices down." He tosses me a key. "For the lift. Fourth floor."

Fourth floor where none of the staff have ever been.

The five players watch me approach Raft and try to steer him.

"Sing him a song," Andy suggests.

"What?" I say.

"The national anthem," Frenchie deadpans.

"A lullaby," Andy says.

"Oh, sweet Jesus." The Piper shakes his head.

"Shut up," Red whispers hoarsely. "The sooner he's back in bed the sooner we can return to the game."

"Rock-a-bye Baby," I mumble. "On a tree-top/when the wind blows the cradle will rock/when the bough breaks the cradle will fall/down will come baby, cradle and all."

The melody seems to penetrate Raft's fog. He allows me to take his arm and lead him back across the room.

"I would appreciate it if no one ever mentions his appearance here tonight." Andy says. "Or his condition."

"We won't breathe a word," Red says. "Will we, fellas?"

It's obvious when Red speaks, everybody listens. The others all make the correct noises.

I coax Raft back up the stairs and into the lift. His key is in the lock, so I don't need Andy's. I hit four and the machinery cranks into action.

I sing mindless sentences softly as they come to my mind.

The lift cranks upwards, terminating with a drop and a lurch. Raft wakes and lifts his head. "Where am I?" he says, groggily.

"In the lift." I lower myself to my haunches. "You were sleep walking."

He wrenches his dressing gown closed.

"Who saw me?" His voice is strangled.

His intense green eyes are full of sorrow. I realise it was Raft I saw peering down the afternoon of my staged interview.

"Just me," I lie. "I heard the lift and came to investigate."

He looks relieved.

"Is the game still on?"

"Yes. They're so involved that no one heard a thing. I doubt they even know I'd left."

"Thank goodness," he says. "Do you know who I am?"

I pretend to guess. "A friend of Andy's?"

"We've been together for 15 years." He sighs. "You could call me the silent partner of this operation."

"Well, pleased to meet you, silent partner."

"I know I can trust you," he lifts his hair and shows off his profile. "Look closely. Are you sure you don't recognise me?"

"Wow," I say. "Aren't you Raft?"

"Yes," he groans.

"You're supposed to be missing."

"I am missing!"

The lift door opens onto a tiled terrace and the skylight dome.

As he steps out his left foot catches on the gap between the floors and I have to catch his arm to steady him.

"Dead leg." He punches his thigh.

A gravelled path lined with hundreds of potted cacti and succulents leads across the terrace to a low, flat-roofed, bungalow fronted by a wall of glass.

"It's like a desert," I say.

"They're the only things that'll grow in this roof environment."

I help him to the entrance, and say, "I should get back. Before I left, Andy and the Pied Piper were playing for Johnnie."

"The Piper was never going to let Johnnie go so easily," Raft says. "He's too much of an asset."

"Why does Andy play for people?"

"Second chances," he says. "To free people of their servitude to those like the Pied Piper."

"Does Nic know?"

"Yes," Raft says. "Nic's known all along."

"I'm glad I'm one of the lucky ones," I say.

"Did you know we met before?" he says. "You won't remember because I was wearing a hooded mask. That disguise disgusts me now. The fact I hid myself to scatter my friend's ashes. All for the sake of protecting my career."

"Quoll!" I say. "I do remember. You gave me money."

"I've traced your movements ever since. When you fell into the clutches of the French banker it became time for Andy to invite him to the game."

"How did you know Quoll?"

"He was my best friend from school," Raft sighs, "He knew everything about me."

Andy Flanagan exits the lift and walks towards the bungalow entrance.

"So, this is where you got to," he says.

"He found me asleep in the lift and returned me safely before anyone saw," Raft says. "I'm indebted forever."

I watch Andy's face as he gets the picture.

"How did the game go?" I say.

"We won," Andy lifts Raft's hand and presses the back of it to his lips. "Johnnie will never be on the table again. Neither will Nic. Neither will you."

.19.

The Countess pulls her hand from the jar. "Dumb bells!" she exclaims, shaking her head.

"What do the dumb bells stand for?"

She laughs, "The Hygiene Party."

"You told me not to be so literal," I say.

"Under normal circumstances," she smiles. "but sometimes even the cufflinks have no choice."

"We haven't had any Hygiene Party goons down here for a while," Nic says.

"Word must have gotten around you underpour their drinks," the Countess laughs.

"Desperate times call for desperate measures."

"Can you underpour the guy who designed the Grim Reaper ad?" I say.

"I do," Nic says. "But he's so full of himself he's never noticed."

"And he always tips big," the Countess chimes in.

*

"I know I was won in a card game," I say to Nic as he ties my Rookwood knot. "I know you were too. Was it from the Pied Piper?"

He smiles, "You think I was a whore?"

"No! No!"

"Nothing against whoredom," Nic says. "There have been whores in every day and age. It's the world's second oldest profession after tending bar."

"Then who?"

"My owner was the Governor," Nic says, "He got me early release and held my probation over me."

"You were in prison?" I say.

155

The Countess stops counting.

"Nic stabbed my husband," she says. "Who was a thug and a bully."

"Is he…?"

"Dead?" she says. "Yes. Good riddance."

"The Governor lost me to Andy," Nic says. "He tried to win me back until he realised he had an entire prison of men at his disposal."

.20.

"What are you going to wear?" I nod at one of the Sleaze Ball posters that've been plastered all over Oxford Street.

"Do we have to dress up?" Ty grumbles.

"It makes it more fun," Johnnie says, arranging himself on his crutches. "My options are limited seeing my leg will still be in a cast."

"How 'bout a wounded soldier boy?" I say. "That's a hot look."

"Ya reckon?" Ty says. "Aren't there enough stupid boys dressed up as soldiers these days?"

"We could go in drag?" I say.

"I'd make an ugly woman," Johnnie says.

"Me too," Ty says. "Let's go as trippy hippies covered in flowers and peace signs."

"Hippies aren't sleazy, are they?" Johnnie says.

Ty adopts a voice of an authoritarian do-gooder. "Free love is filthy and disgusting!"

"Yeah!" Johnnie laughs. "Make the bastards pay."

"Now there's the man I know and love," Ty says.

Four

.1.

Johnnie dances across the room in time to David Bowie singing 'Fashion' on the tape player and waves his hand in front of my mouth. "Open sesame."

"What for?"

"Half a trip."

"I'll pay for the cab," I say, washing down the acid infused paper.

Ty's gazing at himself in the mirror of Johnnie's loft with big silly plastic glasses that take over half his face. "Should I wear these?"

"You look like one of the Banana Splits," I say.

"I loved that show when I was a little kid," Johnnie says breaking into the theme tune. "Na Na Na. Na Na Na, Na."

"So that's a 'na' then." Ty discards the glasses.

The three of us wear long straight hippy wigs, head bands, necklaces and peace signs. Johnnie has entwined his crutches in fake flowers and plastic vines.

"We look great," I say. "Are we ready to hit the road?"

"Ready!"

We head for the taxi rank on Oxford Street.

Johnnie lowers himself onto the backseat and drags himself across while Ty takes his flower adorned crutches and slides in after him. I hop in the front. "To the Royal Sydney Showgrounds, driver! Pronto!" I say. "We've got a party to go to."

The woman starts the meter and angles the car into the traffic. A large silver cross hanging from the rear vision mirror starts swinging with the motion. "I'm not breaking any road rules for you," she declares. "There's enough rules being broken tonight."

"What rules are those?" Ty says.

The driver leans forward and turns up the radio volume on a round-table discussion.

...as we speak, they're holding what they call the Sleaze Ball at the Royal Sydney Showgrounds where good Christian families go to attend the Royal Easter Show. Now I ask you, how can we be sure that gay plague isn't going to be lurking in the woodwork waiting to pounce on our innocent children when they go to purchase showbags?

The radio host butts in, *Good point.*

Ty lets out a laugh in the backseat. "Oh, Jesus."

The driver locks her eyes on him in the rear vision mirror. "Watch your mouth."

The City of Sydney should change its name to the City of Degeneracy, states another attendee.

Another man interjects: *have we learnt nothing? It's Sodom and Gomorrah all over again! Those two cities as it states in Jude 1:7 that 'gave themselves up to sexual immorality and serve as an example of those who suffer the punishment of eternal fire'.*"

"Can you turn that off?" I say.

"Get out and walk if you can't handle the truth," the woman says. "I fill my ears with the word of God when the devil's on the prowl."

Johnnie sighs and rolls down his window. "If the devil's on the prowl then we're sitting ducks in this traffic jam. What in hell's name is going on with all these road works?"

"God's placed a roadblock in our path to make us reconsider our lifestyle," Ty says. "Isn't that right driver?"

Again, she trains her eyes on him in the rear vision mirror.

"Flee from sexual immorality," she says. "All other sins a person commits are outside the body, but whoever sins sexually, sins against their own body. 1 Corinthians 6:18."

The cab creeps forward.

"You've a good memory for scripture. Here's one I remember from when I was a boy," Ty says. "Do you recall this one Johnnie? I do not permit a woman to teach or to assume authority over a man; she must be quiet. 1 Timothy 2:12. But you know what? I don't believe that either."

Johnnie shushes him. "She'll kick us out and I don't want to walk."

Ty shrugs. "She started it."

Finally, we arrive.

"Hallelujah," Ty says.

I hand over a 20 and wait for the change as Ty holds the door open for Johnnie to manoeuvre his way out.

Careful not to touch my skin the driver places the coins one by one into my palm. "1 Corinthians 6:19. Do you not know that your bodies are temples of the Holy Spirit, who is in you, whom you have received from God? You are not your own; you were bought at a price. Therefore, honour God with your bodies."

"I plan to," I reply, bitchily. "With as many men as I can. Consider that your tip."

She snarls, "Judgement Day is coming and when it comes it's going to break on your head! Consider that yours!"

Her tongue transforms. A fist punches from her mouth. The fist rotates and opens. It's the Countess's white hand holding a teetering pile of bones collapsing off the edges. My eyes follow the falling bones into the footwell where they collect and multiply up to my calves. Bone fingers scuttle and point. It's the LSD. I can't get out of the car quick enough.

"Hey, shut the door!"

Behind the cab a large group of dykes pour out of a minibus, wearing over-drawn curlicue moustaches, top hats and tails, some are wearing no trousers.

A top hat slams the door for me. "I've got it old chap!"

The crowd crams 10-deep at the turnstiles. Multi-coloured tinsel, feathers and scales delineate fantasy creatures of land, air and sea. There's an over-load of plucked and shaven flesh. So blatant. So raw. Like meat waiting for a pitchfork. My eyes carry infection from the taxi driver. I try to rub away the visions, but the drugs are too strong. Arms become undulating pythons and faces distort into howler monkeys. I see several Grim Reapers moving through the crowd and don't know if they're real.

I follow Ty and Johnnie into the throng before the visions become unbearable.

Ty registers the look on my face. "Are you okay?"

"I'm seeing things."

"I am too. Here," he says, "take my hand."

*

We promenade around the Sleaze Ball's huge dancefloor to Grace Jones singing 'Slave to the Rhythm'. My body is awash with sensation. I feel I am floating. At least my hallucinations have diminished.

"Let's top up in the toilets," Johnnie says.

The queue is ridiculous, and the piss trough is chock-full of men waiting to relieve themselves. "Disabled person coming through," Johnnie sings out. The crowd parts and he swings through on his crutches. He whistles for Ty and me to follow into the next available cubicle.

The door locked, Johnnie pulls out a little plastic transparent bag and Ty rolls a twenty-dollar bill into a straw. Johnnie wipes the top of the cistern with some toilet paper and lines up three fat lines of speed. Ty snorts first. Johnnie second. Then me. We pinch our noses and hold our heads back.

"It burns," I say. "It's good though."

On the way out we see a man lying in the base of the urinal waiting for men to piss all over him. "Oh my God! I'm hallucinating," I gasp.

"That's Trough Man," Johnnie says.

"Go on," Ty tells me. "Do your community service."

"I'm not pissing on him!"

Johnnie manoeuvres his crutches up onto the platform, pulls out his dick, and aims his stream lazily up and down the length of the man's fully clothed body. The man looks up at him like a supplicant in a religious painting.

I aim for the wall, the taste of speed in the back of my mouth and my heart beating in time to the thump of music. I want to dance.

Brilliant blue lasers fire from every direction and build shimmering moving walls of fantasy castles. Giant mirror balls descend and retract from the ceiling like robotic testicles. I'm speeding off my dial. Johnnie gives me another quarter trip and time is lost. How long have we been here? Two hours? Ten? Ty dances beside me, glistening and sinuous, beads swinging, his hippy wig is plastered with sweat to his neck and shoulders. Eyes closed, he's as far gone as I am. Johnnie rests on his crutches beside one of the giant speaker boxes. He waves a bottle of amyl, his arm undulating like a snake. I shimmy over and accept what's on offer. His eyes glow with something like phosphorescence. Even though I've known him forever, I'm stunned by how good he looks. Everyone is.

"You look amazzzzzingg," I say as I jam the small brown bottle to my nose and snort in the fumes. Johnnie smiles beatifically.

The Royal Hall of Industries is an animal, alive and throbbing with six thousand, near-naked people dancing to the thump, thump, thump, of its beating heart. My body responds to sensation only. Lasers ratchet overhead slicing the foggy drifts of cigarette smoke, body heat, and dry ice. Stomping dancers blow silver whistles like cicadas in a kaleidoscopic forest. The air is heavy with a warm soup of marijuana, cologne, cigarettes, sweat, and the soft smell of talcum powder shaken onto the floor panels by moustachioed clones so they can fan dance like birds of paradise.

The Sisters of Perpetual Indulgence swoop like magpies around a flotilla of grand old drags in treacherous heels navigating the shoals of abandoned cups and beer cans on the perimeter of the dance floor, before zooming off.

Song melts into song. Sucked and moved by waves of sound I'm dancing with no one and everyone. There's no self in this being. I'm at one with everybody.

Ty, circled by a group of mates from the Aboriginal and Islander Dance Company, starts dancing like nothing I've ever seen. Like he's been waiting to dance his entire life and everything else he's done has been just keeping the engine warm.

Johnnie, above all physical pain now, abandons his crutches and climbs atop a six-foot high speaker box without help. Dropping his hippy vest and his long hippy wig, he reveals himself to the crowd. Recognition fires in onlookers' eyes. *It's Johnnie. Our Most Beautiful. Saint Johnnie.* Muscle men, their eyes ablaze with drugged love, surround the speaker box. Johnnie spreads his arms like he's Jesus Christ. He falls and is swept up. He's in ecstasy as he's passed overhead from one adoring group to the next. We're all in ecstasy. Bodies intertwined in a mad garden. Eyes and teeth glitter like jewels. We are beautiful and savage.

Lights flare and the music wrenches to a stop. Dumbfounded, I shield my eyes.

A voice booms.

"ATTENTION: DUE TO THE ONGOING HYGIENE EMERGENCY THIS PARTY IS CANCELLED. FOLLOW INSTRUCTIONS AND YOU WON'T GET HURT."

A howl of disbelief erupts.

Then a dawning question: who won't get hurt?

"MALES AND FEMALES WILL SPLIT INTO TWO GROUPS, NO EXCEPTION. GUARDS ARE STATIONED TO CHECK. FEMALES WILL EXIT THROUGH THE LEFT DOOR AND MALES TO THE RIGHT."

They can't forcibly check, can they? Absolutely not.

I hear the sound of barking dogs as the doors facing Moore Park are flung open. Men yell through loud hailers, "MOVE!"

Ty appears by my side wild-eyed, saying, "Where's Johnnie?"

There is no sign of him.

"Stay here." Ty scrambles to the top of the stadium-seating to scan the crowd.

A whip-crack sound jolts the frightened crowd. Gunshot? People scream.

"Thank God you're here," I say as Johnnie hobbles back from wherever he landed.

"Where's Ty?"

I point. "Up there looking for you."

Johnnie waves his arms to get Ty's attention. "I'm scared."

"Me too. Stay here while I get your stuff."

I get Johnnie's vest and crutches. Ty pushes his way back through the tide of moving bodies.

"What did you see from up there?" Johnnie says.

"Hygiene Party goons dressed for a fight," he says, grimly. "With your leg it'll be easier if we move behind the bleachers and make our way along the wall."

A different beat starts up. Baton against breastplate.

"MOVE!"

Amyl bottles and drug paraphernalia are dropped and crushed. A pungent chemical smell fills the air. I see a panicked young drag queen kick off her stilettos and abandon her wig.

"Keep your shoes on or you'll cut your feet," scolds an older queen as she picks her way disdainfully through the detritus.

The young one ignores her.

The voice screams "EVACUATE NOW!"

Ty is right about the path behind the bleachers. We hear batons thwack as Johnnie swings between us on his crutches like a metronome. It's slow going but at least we're not being jostled or separated by others. My hallucinations are subsiding but when I look to the ceiling it's scuttling and alive with all sorts of scaled and winged invertebrates. It's just the play of light, it's just the play of light I tell myself, lowering my eyes and concentrating on the flowers painted on Johnnie's plaster cast. We stall at the river of women bottlenecked at their designated door. We must cross to reach the male exit.

"MOVE. MOVE. MOVE."

Screams ring out.

They're hitting people.

Fed by fear, the women heave forward. Eyes skitter, the screaming intensifies, people strain for air. I can smell piss.

Women at the front are trying to turn back. One of them yells, "Go back! People are being crushed!"

"KEEP MOVING," screams the voice. "OR FACE THE CONSE-QUENCES."

A gunshot cracks. The plug of women at the doorway mouth explodes like a champagne cork, heaving the women behind them down the stairs. With an exhausted groan the crowd starts to tumble through, climbing over the fallen ones.

"This is insane," Johnnie cries.

"And deliberate," Ty says. 'They're shell-shocking us."

A horrible space appears between the injured and those pushing, as if the crowd recoils from the damage it is doing.

"Cross!" Ty shouts. "Now!"

He holds his arms like a traffic warden to ensure Johnnie navigates across safely.

"MOVE. MOVE. MOVE."

With a wailing heave the clearway closes, but we have made it through to the leeway between the two thronging sexes, an indeterminate zone filled with those who can't decide. Transsexuals done up like Vegas showgirls shriek, "Which group?" Some are weeping, others curse, everyone is afraid of what waits outside.

The crush of men we now confront makes me think of stinking cattle being forced up an abattoir gangway. Faces so recently transfixed in ecstasy now twist in panic, eyes rolling. A man reaches from the mass pleading, "Help, I can't breathe."

Gunfire crackles. "MOVE! MOVE! MOVE!"

The man who can't breathe is suddenly propelled forward. Again, the crowd recoils.

"Go, now!" Ty yells.

"I dropped a crutch!" Johnnie wails.

"Grab them!" Ty yells at me.

I do, and Ty sweeps Johnnie up in his arms and is halfway down the steps before Johnnie can argue. I follow as he miraculously finds spaces between the broken and bloodied bodies and outstretched hands. "I'm sorry. I'm sorry," I sob as the surge we have joined tramples them.

We are out and blinded by the glare of floodlights. The thud of generators echoes my racing heart. Leering white-painted faces jostle forward. Warm gobs of spit hit my face. I am hit in the back by a baton to keep moving. Ty yells. He is still carrying Johnnie and they're both taking baton hit after baton hit. I rush forward with the crutches. Around us, drag queens separated out by cattle prods have hoses turned on them and I see The Sisters of Perpetual Indulgence being herded into the back of a truck, the white of their habits now splattered red. I see the young drag queen who'd kicked away her shoes with bloodied feet, hear the older one, still trying to chaperone, call, "Keep your head high and…"

She is drowned out by a goon wielding a loud hailer snarling, "KEEP MOVING. KEEP YOUR HEADS DOWN. LOITERERS WILL BE PUNISHED."

Funnelled between two rows of baton wielders we are swallowed by the machinery of hate. The sound from the generators dampens the screams coming from behind us.

A middle-aged man in leather chaps breaks from the funnelling to accost a man wearing the greatest amount of insignia on the lapels of his Hygiene Party uniform.

"What is the meaning of this?" he demands. "By whose authority?"

He crumbles to the ground under a flurry of baton blows.

Bondi is one of the bashers. I recognise the same sneer from the cliff pathway. Dropping my eyes, I quicken my pace.

Johnnie says through chattering teeth, "Where are we going?"

"To hell," Ty says. "But we've been there together before and survived, Johnnie, right?"

"Right." Johnnie swallows a sob.

There is no sign of the women as we are herded away from the showgrounds and across Moore Park. No light shines from the facing terrace houses.

A young guy covered in gold glitter paint and wearing nothing but a Tarzan flap nods at Ty.

"Who's that?" Johnnie says shakily.

"Daryl," Ty says. "He's one of the Aboriginal dancers."

"He's hot," Johnnie says.

"Really? We're herded by freaks with guns and dogs and you're still thinking with your dick? You're unbelievable."

Johnnie laughs weakly. "I'll be thinking with my dick on my deathbed."

"Look." I point to where it looks like the dawn is glimmering. But the glare ahead becomes too harsh and white to be the sun.

Taylor Square is no longer recognisable. Harsh spotlights illuminate hastily erected fifteen-foot-high, barbed-wire-topped concrete panels that wall off the surrounding buildings. Guard towers set up on semi-trailers flank the new entrance that we're being fed into.

I recognise a man from Lana's building pointing at our apartments outside the perimeter and beseeching, "I live right there. This is a dreadful mistake. I've got work on Monday."

He is smashed into line.

.2.

Floodlights. Guns. Batons. Thumping generators and the stink of diesel. Snarling handlers and barking dogs. Hate. Covertly, I register the position of each guard in relation to my own. I may have been hopeless at school, but I'm adept at this type of trigonometry. This is me calculating my proximity to my stepfather to escape being hit. I see people struck and pummelled because they don't know how to keep their heads down, but the three of us do. Smart, instinctively self-protective, we move and act similarly, ears straining, eyes locked on the dividing line on the bitumen: we're fed through the gap in the wall.

The sounds of yelling and beating falls behind. Through, and past the worst, we fan out exhausted. "No, no, no!" A high thin voice leaps up behind us as a little rotund man is pulled out of the line and frog marched into the palm trees on Gilligan's Island where he is viciously beaten. There's nothing anyone can do.

"Keep walking," Ty says quietly. "Get away from the gate."

We come upon the wounded lying moaning in their party costumes in front of shuttered Oxford Street shops.

"Call an ambulance." A man cradling another in a doorway calls desperately. "Call an ambulance."

"His mate's clearly dead," Ty says under his breath. "There's nothing we can do. "Keep going."

"But where to?" Johnnie says.

"Your place," Ty says. "You're an easy target on those crutches. We need to get you off the street."

My hallucinations have completely stopped. It's as if the LSD can't dream up anything worse than the awful reality. My eyes linger on an older blond man hunched on the footpath. He holds a white construction helmet that's smeared with blood. His lower jaw hangs obscenely.

"What are you doing?" Ty says.

"I have to help him," I answer. "I can't keep walking past."

"We've got to get Johnnie home."

"You go on, I'll catch up."

Johnnie manoeuvres his crutches in my direction. "We'll wait. We're not splitting up."

I drop to my haunches and peer into the injured man's eyes.

He's wearing jeans and a sleeveless pale blue denim shirt. His gold sunglasses have a lost lens.

Despite the damage I recognise him.

"Hey, Construction Worker, didn't I see you at the Ball with a group of friends dressed as The Village People?"

His eyes return to focus but fill with pain as he nods.

I glance about. "Where are they?"

The Construction Worker's shoulders lift and sag.

I climb to my feet, "We'll find them for you, okay?"

"Talk about looking for a needle in a bloody haystack," Johnnie says. "There's a thousand leathermen, soldiers and construction worker clones crammed in here with us."

"Search for the Indian," Ty says. "That's a harder look to pull off."

Johnnie lowers himself beside the injured man and arranges his crutches alongside. "I'll keep him company while you find Felipe. We might even have a singalong to cheer ourselves up."

"Don't go anywhere," Ty says as we move back into the tide of shuffling exhausted bodies. Behind us we hear Johnnie's voice lift over our heads, timid at first but gaining in power.

"Can he sing?' I ask Ty.

"Nope," Ty says. Johnnie's voice sounds sweet and trying, but the words are drowned by the cries and entreaties of people pushing past us.

"What's he singing?"

"I think it's 'Can't Stop the Music'," Ty says.

There is a lull in the noise around us and I hear it. I start to sing, too. A couple of other voices join, then the song erupts like every C-grade movie we've ever laughed about in the pub, or on the phone, or at Bill & Toni's.

We hear cries of recognition from where we left Johnnie.

We backtrack through the crowd to find a bunch of Village People looka-likes gazing down at their injured friend. There's the G.I., the Cop, the Leatherman, Cowboy, and Felipe sans his feather headdress. He must have abandoned it to lessen the attention.

Johnnie hauls himself to his feet and swings himself over. "Mission accomplished!"

"Like moths to a flame," Ty says.

"I wish one was a doctor," I say as we move on with the tide, past a clot of people lining up to drink from a firehose someone has unfurled from one of the buildings.

At the intersection of Crown and Oxford Street, Carmen Miranda – pale green plastic grapes still plastered to the side of her head – directs invisible vehicles as if she's a traffic cop. A fan dancer flutters about her flicking his fans open and closed. Beyond them, Centrepoint Tower glints in the early morning sunlight, cold and impervious.

From somewhere nearby a voice crackles out of a loud hailer: "a first aid station is being set up at the crown street post office. repeat: a first aid station is being set up at the crown street post office. any medical professionals please attend asap."

"At least somebody knows what to do," I say.

"Gays are good in an emergency," Ty says. "It's not our first time at the rodeo."

I gaze up Crown Street to the new wall that's cut us off from the Oriental Hotel. Soldiers stare down from a newly erected guard tower. In the other direction another wall cuts down the middle of Stanley Street.

"No more Bill and Toni's," I lament.

"Their coffee was too hot anyway," Johnnie grins.

"I've been expecting something like this to happen my entire life," I say, "but how the hell did they manage to put these walls up so quickly?"

"Would have had everything ready to go," Ty says.

*

There are less people milling about when we reach my old begging corner opposite the Koala Motor Inn. I debate saying something about once being a street scab but the memory of what I once thought was dangerous and thrilling now seems quaint and irrelevant. Johnnie needs to catch his breath. He lowers himself onto the step where Quoll used to sit.

I think of Nathan, the boy with the red beanie who'd sliced his own throat with my box-cutter, and wonder if his ghost is waiting nearby for the Opera Lady to come and sing him to a higher plane. I wonder how she'll get in now a wall is up.

Johnnie points to a lumpy pile of material fifty metres away in the middle of Riley Street. "Is that a body?"

"Looks like it," I say.

"Should we move him off the road?" Johnnie says.

"Please, Johnnie, that poor guy is past caring. We need to get you home."

I've never heard Ty's voice sound so pleading. The blood has drained from his lips. He looks exhausted. We all are.

I look down Oxford Street to where the wall crosses Whitlam Square three blocks down and see something glint from the top of it. Soldiers, watching us through binoculars.

Raising one of his wooden crutches, Johnnie aims it like a rifle at them. "I hate those guys."

"Don't," I say. "They might think it's an actual gun. Let's go to your place."

Books, clothing, toys lie scattered down Riley Street and up Norman Street. Smashed gates hang off their hinges.

Frantic beckoning from a terrace house doorway attracts our attention.

"That's Mr Westacott," Johnnie murmurs.

"Come in! Hurry!" the old man whispers, making room in his hall. "They came in the middle of the night. Every house!"

"They've built a big wall right around Darlo, Mr Westacott," Johnnie says. "There's armed guards all along it. How come you're still here?"

"I hid!" he says, fiercely. "I couldn't sleep with all the construction noise and lights blarin'. I was wide awake when they came yelling about that hygiene emergency brought on by you lot."

"Where'd you hide?" Johnnie says.

"In the chicken coop," he says. "I could hear 'em dragging people out of their houses all round me!"

"Maybe you should go talk to them, Mr Westacott," Johnnie says. "Take your ID. Tell them you're not a homo."

He shakes his head. "I ain't leavin'. And they better not try me! I've got a few tricks up my sleeve. I used to be in the army you know. Attended two wars. New Guinea and Korea! Things I kept that could still cause a bit of trouble. Mementos, you could call 'em."

Johnnie laughs bleakly. "Now don't go doing anything silly, Mr Westacott."

"You neither lad. You neither. And how 'bout you call me Cyril instead of Mr Westacott. I ain't ya headmaster."

"Righto, Cyril. How about I swing by and check on you in a couple of days. You got everything you need?"

The old man runs his finger down the broken hinge. "I'd be better if they hadn't busted me door down, but I'll be okay."

We continue on past the rear of the Exchange Hotel and the Yurong Street stairs that run up beside it to Oxford Street. In Oxford Lane we pass under the warehouse bridges and approach Johnnie's garage. It looks undamaged. Hand shaking, he slips in the key. He closes and relocks the door and we climb to the mezzanine. Safe, we gather about the little sink and gulp down glassfuls of water.

Johnnie hobbles to the intercom and presses the talk button.

"Andy?" he says.

Andy's voice jumps through. "Thank God, you're alright! Kit and Ty? Are they with you? Anyone hurt?"

A sob escapes Johnnie's throat. "We're okay, but there's dead bodies in the street."

"Try not to think about it. The building is secure. Rest now. Do you need anything? Extra pillows or blankets? I can send Nic down with some."

"We should be fine," Johnnie says.

"Hi Nic!" I call. "Glad you're okay."

"Me too, Kit," Nic says. "See you after you've slept."

We slump on the sofa and Johnnie switches on the television.

The Prime Minister, talking to Ossie Austin, is saying, "Debauchery and hedonism, Ossie. We simply had to put a stop to it."

"As this footage shows," Ossie says.

The camera pans over a vast littered space and a female voice intones, "I'm here at the Sydney Showgrounds and the floor of the Royal Hall of Industries is literally covered with drugs and drug-taking paraphernalia."

The young woman bends to pick up something from the floorboard. She holds up a small bag of white powder.

"This is amphetamine, ladies and gentlemen. Known colloquially as speed, or go-ey." She raises her other hand. "This little brown bottle contains a substance called amyl, or rush. When snorted it's said to heighten sexual pleasure." She shakes her head. "Goodness only knows what really went on here last night, and what we are about to show you now is truly grotesque," she says. "I suggest any children watching should be sent from the room."

The camera changes to a different scene.

Lying in the trough of the male toilets is Trough Man. Fast asleep and soaked through with urine.

The camera returns to the Prime Minister's narrowed eyes: "Our world teeters on the brink of catastrophe and this is how one section of our community chooses to behave? This disgusting celebration of deviant behaviour was the final straw. The government has decided to quarantine these people until they behave in a way more fitting of civilised society."

The television goes to an ad break for The Hygiene Party.

"Turn it off," Ty says. "I've had about all I can take, and I need a shower."

Johnnie kills the television. "I do too but I'm scared I'll fall over."

"I'll hold ya," Ty says. "We can shower together."

Johnnie looks at me.

"You two go ahead," I say.

I watch them undress and manoeuvre under the hot stream in the shower cubicle. I've never seen Ty completely naked. He's beautiful. At first they are businesslike as they begin to soap one another. No words are spoken. Then they begin to kiss. Johnnie lowers himself to his knees and takes Ty in his mouth. He climbs back up and they hug and let the water envelop their bodies. They beckon me. I drop my clothes and move into their open arms through the steam. It's comfort and it's necessary. A way to right some of the wrong. We've survived.

Later, in bed, our bodies touching, I focus on the pale orange spheres moving across my closed eyelids and think of the ghosts lining Oxford Street. The memory of the Opera Lady's song soothes all thought, sound, and image away.

.3.

"Wake up fellas!" Nic's voice. "Dinner in twenty. Get dressed and come to the cellar. The table's set up."

I'm on Johnnie's couch under a blanket. The bed was too small for three bodies. It's early evening and we've slept all day. Last night wasn't a dream.

The intercom clicks off. I call, "Why the cellar?"

"No one can see or hear us there," Johnnie says.

Ty sits up yawning.

"How do you feel?" I ask. "You took a lot of baton whacks getting us out last night."

Ty gingerly touches the welts on his shoulders. "I'll be okay."

I stand on tingling legs, cross to the windows and crack open the heavy curtain. Torrential rain. I picture the cold body lying in the middle of Riley Street and quickly try to remove the image from my mind.

"There's no way I'm wearing what I wore last night," I say. "Have you got anything else?"

"There's shirts and jeans in the cupboard," Johnnie says. "Help yourselves."

Walking to the cellar along the hidden passageway through the back of the garage, Johnnie says, "Andy owns this whole block, but rents the majority out."

"Rich bastard," Ty mutters.

Three bar tables have been pushed together and set with cutlery and napkins. A candelabra throws wavering light over the stacked boxes of alcohol, beer, and chips. A portable radio plays in the background. Andy appears, carrying the food.

My mouth waters as he places roast chickens in the middle of the table interspersed with bowls of salad and baskets of little buttered bread rolls.

"This looks cosy," Johnnie says.

"We've got to get rid of the perishables," Andy says. "There've been two blackouts already."

Ty says to me quietly, "Six chairs. Who else is coming?"

Andy overhears. "My partner. I don't think you've met."

Ty looks questioningly at Johnnie and me. We feign ignorance.

Nic arrives, his head bandaged.

"What happened to you?" I exclaim.

"Mongrels hit me from behind."

"Where's the Countess?"

"Hopefully on the outside. After you left work to go get ready for the party we closed up and went home to Da's. Then the trucks came. They knew who to take and who to leave. I was arguing with her to go with Da and that's the last I remember. I came to on the footpath."

"Has she been in touch? Has she rung?"

"The phones are dead."

Raft appears. He wears an emerald dinner jacket, and his thick Clarke Gablesque hair is slicked back.

Andy introduces him to Ty who looks stunned as he shakes the hand of the 'missing' movie star. "Pleased to meet you finally, Ty," Raft smiles broadly. "I've heard a lot about you."

Ty can only nod.

We sit with Andy and Raft at opposite ends like Mum and Dad. Wine is poured, chicken carved and plated. Cloth napkins unfurl.

Andy raises his glass. "I'd like to make a toast and welcome Ty to the Burdekin. I just wish it was under better circumstances."

"Welcome Ty!"

Ty mumbles his thanks over the clink of glasses.

An ad weaves out of the radio. A concerned female voice saying: *Is there someone in your community you find yourself wondering about? Someone who presents in a way that seem at odds with the way you live your life? Trust your instincts. These individuals could be the vessels that carry the gay plague into the heart of your community. Don't take that chance. Ring now. Your call is toll-free with complete anonymity assured. Dob in a Deviant.*

Raft says in a flat voice, "Can we turn that off?"

"What if we miss something?" Nic says.

"You'd get more reliable information reading the entrails of that bird in front of you," Raft says. "It's propaganda for the Hygiene Party, that and the damn Grim Reaper ad."

Nic leans back and dials the volume down.

Andy raises his glass again. "If I may continue, I'd also like to take this opportunity and thank our lucky stars that you're all safe and well, despite a couple of dings. May our luck continue!"

"May our luck continue!"

Again, our glasses clink.

"Now eat up!"

Shovelling food in my mouth I remember my stepfather's fists and I think about how vastly different dinner used to be at home. Swallowing, I put down my knife and fork.

"May I say something?"

"Go right ahead," Andy says.

"Despite everything that's happened outside I'm glad I'm here with you all. You are my family."

Mouths full, clatter of cutlery, my dinner companions raise their glasses one more time, "Hear, hear!"

*

"How was the Ball?" Nic reaches for another helping.

"Brilliant," I say. "Before the soldiers came and turned it into bedlam."

"They're not soldiers, they're brain-washed lunatics!" Raft breaks into a coughing fit.

We wait for him to regain his composure and then try and recap the horror of the night. Johnnie describes the body we saw in the street. "He must still be out there lying in the rain."

180

Nic shoves out his chair and says quietly, "I have to go and collect him. It's my job to collect the bodies now that Da's not here. I'll take out the hearse. There's no one else."

"You can't go out there in your condition," Raft admonishes. "You've got a head injury."

"Da wouldn't let that stop him, yet here I am hiding like a rat in the cellar."

"Now that's enough," Andy says. "You're concussed."

Ty speaks up. "I'll go with him."

"Wait," I say. "The Countess would consult the cufflinks if she were here. As she did at the start of every shift, to forecast the night ahead."

"Did she forecast the wall?" Ty says.

"Yes, I think so," I say, "The last cufflink she pulled broke apart in her hand and she said, 'The world split in two.' But she couldn't decipher its meaning."

"Get the cufflinks, Kit," Nic says. "She said you had a touch of the prescient."

"She did? She never told me."

I retrieve the jar from where it's stored beneath the bar, roll it back and forth as I'd seen the Countess do, and unscrew the lid.

At the last moment I baulk. "Someone else pick."

"Who?" Johnnie says.

I point to Ty. Nic and Andy nod.

"What?" Ty says as I place the jar before him.

"Pull out the first thing you touch."

Ty puts his knife and fork down and crosses his arms. "Why me? You think because I'm Aboriginal I've got special powers? Or are you trying to suck me into the Andy Gang? Either way, the answer's no."

"Duly noted. Ty is NOT part of the Andy Gang." Smiling, Andy pretends to scribble words on an invisible piece of paper.

"Sorry Ty," I say. "You're right. I ask too much. The only reason we survived last night was because of you."

"It's true," Johnnie says. "You carried me out of Sleaze Ball."

Ty's arms uncross.

I take a cufflink from the bottle and put it on the tablecloth. Everyone leans in.

Nic whistles through his teeth. "Scarab beetle. The one cufflink that always eluded my sister." His eyes glitter. "The cufflinks have spoken."

"But what does scarab mean?" Johnnie says.

"My father," Nic says.

"This is ridiculous!" Raft says. "It's the middle of the night. What are those goons going to think of you rolling about the streets in that fancy black trap?"

"The Kinselas funeral wagon is this city's most recognisable vehicle," Andy says. "Especially since the funeral of Mrs Evelyn Gatt. They'll know what we're doing."

"What do you mean by we?" Raft says to him. "You can't possibly think you're going?"

"Of course." Andy dabs the sides of his mouth with his napkin. "Nic has a potential concussion and we can't leave it all up to these young lads if something goes wrong, despite Ty's proven capabilities."

"It's called being a mate," Ty mutters.

"Ease off, Ty," Johnnie says. "You gotta learn to take a compliment."

"Where will we take the bodies?" I say.

"To the funeral parlour," Nic says. "Da keeps the key in the cart."

"Who else is going on this fool's errand?" Raft says.

"Not you, or Johnnie," Andy says.

"Can't I at least drive you to the stables?" Johnnie almost whines.

"The car remains hidden," Andy says. "Goons dragged all the other motor vehicles off the street to stop escape attempts probably. In fact, we should dismantle her and hide the parts."

"I'll start while you're gone," Johnnie says. "I won't feel so useless."

"We'll need gloves and raincoats," Ty says.

"Follow me," Johnnie gets up from the table. "There's wet weather gear under the car's front seat."

"I guess that leaves me to clean up this mess," Raft grumbles.

.4.

From the wall at Taylor Square down to the wall at Whitlam Square, all the traffic lights flash on amber. Spotlights claw at the heavy cloud and a siren wails from somewhere down on Stanley. Ty grabs my arm. Following Nic and Andy, we bolt across to my old scabbing corner and dash up Arnold Place towards Crown until Nic says, "Down!"

We crouch behind bins as a truck full of goons speeds through the intersection headed for the Campbell Street wall.

We race across to the Gaslight Inn and up Little Oxford Street; the lane running parallel to its namesake. Belongings are spread over the roadway as if vomited from the open doorways.

Nic's dad's place is a cottage with a side driveway that leads to the stables. Nic carefully picks up a crushed lipstick canister and a broken-backed photograph album with loose photos displayed like a hand of cards and places them on the porch.

Leading us up the driveway he pulls the bolts on the stable's double doors and drags them open. The rich warm smell of horse and hay rolls out.

"How long has your family been in the funeral business?" Andy says.

"Eons," Nic says.

Ty slowly approaches the two black horses in the stalls. He lays his hand against one flat cheek. "What are their names?"

"Da wanted something like Daisy, or Rosie, but my sister Tess named them Psycho, and Pomp."

Nic regards our questioning looks.

"In Greek mythology Psychopomp was a guide to the spirit world," he says. "Tess split the word in two. Pomp is the darker of the two."

"The Countess is never obvious," Andy says. "She could have called them River and Styx."

Nic laughs and shakes his head. "That was my suggestion."

Nic feeds and dresses the horses in their wet weather gear, harnesses them to the funeral carriage, and leads them out into the laneway. He lights the lamps, fits them to each corner of the carriage, climbs into his seat and jams on his father's top hat.

The rain has stopped.

"This is my world," he says. "Things must be done my way. Agreed?"

Andy bows his head and Ty and I nod.

Nic hoists the wooden handled bell, "I need a ringer."

"Like the harbinger of doom?" Ty says. "No thanks."

"Pass," Andy says. "It'll play havoc with my tinnitus."

Nic's eyes fall on me. "Every twelve steps ring it with slow heft, so it sounds like So Long. So Long. So Long."

He demonstrates. I'm suddenly back behind the bar being taught how to count the free-pour, and know this job was meant for me. I'll always be his apprentice.

Nic turns to Andy and Ty. "Your job is to sweep the rubbish away from the horses." he points. "Grab those brooms."

We start our slow procession. I count to twelve and ring the bell. It has the same tone as my old school's recess bell.

So Long. So Long. So Long.

I recall the scattering of Quoll's ashes. Now I'm the bell ringer.

Men exit the laneway houses where they've sought refuge from the elements and stand heads bowed. Ty and Andy scoot ahead brushing aside broken glass and anything else that may cause problems. We turn in a wide arc onto Crown and then onto Oxford. Streetlights bathe the entire intersection in smoky gold. The wagon looks regal, as if from a coronation, or a monarch's funeral. Rags of mist hanging beneath the shop awnings seem to glide forward. I see features in their soft contours. Hollow cheeks, sad mouths, and eyes.

Every twelve steps I ring the bell. *So Long. So Long. So Long.* People appear in the windows along both sides of Oxford Street. A man runs across from

The Community Resource Centre and falls into step.

"I'm Eddie from the Emergency Response Committee," he calls. "Are you headed to the Koala Motor Inn?"

"No," Nic says politely. "There's a body on Riley Street that we're going to take to Kinselas. Why?"

"The Koala's been converted into a hospital and they've got two bodies that they don't know what to do with."

"We'll attend the Koala after."

"How do we contact you when we hear of others?"

When, not if.

"Slip a note under the door of the Burdekin Hotel," Nic calls, "They know how to find me."

"If you're hungry there's food at the Koala," the man calls, peeling away. "A fella called Betty is setting up a soup kitchen."

No longer impeded by rain, a spotlight from the wall at the Hyde Park end pins us like the finger of doom.

"Should we stop?" Andy calls.

"It's obvious we're the funeral wagon," Nic says. "Ring the bell."

So Long. So Long. So Long.

As we turn into Riley Street past 'old scab corner' we slip out of the spotlight's beam. On the left, Quoll's old apartment building looms into cloud.

So Long. So Long. So Long.

Most apartments are in darkness. The few occupants left hide behind covered windows. On the right, stretches the hoarding surrounding the building site for the proposed new police station. The streetlight, always weak in this area, now seems non-existent.

The horses clip clop down towards a curious flatness, black as a void. The body has disappeared. As we get closer the soft glow from the lamps reveals water filling the lowest point of the street.

"Jesus," Andy says. "The Slough of Despond."

Nic pulls the animals to a halt. "I'm not driving the horses into that."

"The drain must be blocked." Ty rolls up his pants legs.

"I'll help," I say.

"That water has death in it. Keep your shoes on and wear your gloves." Nic riffles through the seat compartment and tosses Ty a torch, "Take this."

Ty turns the beam on the water's surface and finds the curve of the dead body's shoulder. The rest lies hidden. Stepping carefully we search along the gutter for the blockage. Ty uses the handle of his broom to poke ahead. The water is knee-deep. Ripples move out across the surface and break against the body lying like an island in a midnight sea.

Ty shines the torch down into the water revealing soft coral shapes and colours.

"What are they?" I say.

"Silk cushions," Ty says.

Plane tree leaves stick to them like starfish. Ty hands me the torch, seizes one and flings it over the apartment block's front fence. A facecloth flares up like a stingray. Little sucking whirlpools open on the surface near where the drain is emptying. The whirlpools get bigger as the detritus swept here by the rain is removed. A shaggy mat, like an animal pelt, proves to be the final obstacle. The draining sounds like gagging. I grab a doll by its fat little arm and lift it out of the stew. I remember Frenchie calling me a doll on a stick. One that no one would pick up once it fell. Feeling sorry for the sodden thing I slosh across to the entryway of Quoll's tower and cram her in the balustrades. "You'll be safe there," I whisper.

"That shouldn't take too long to empty," Ty says as we make our way back to the carriage while flinging aside any potential further blockages.

"Good job, fellas," Nic says.

Andy gazes at the hoarding surrounding the building site, each panel marked with the same set of black stencilled words **Bill Posters Will Be Prosecuted** on which several Sleaze Ball posters have been defiantly posted. "Well I can't see how they're going to build the new police station with the wall going up."

"Oh, too bad," Ty says.

"In this town you can slay a man and leave his body in the street," Andy says. "But you can still get prosecuted for glue and a bit of paper."

"Yup," Ty says. "The world's gone crazy. Kangaroos in the top paddock crazy."

"Not just kangaroos," Andy says. "Cassowaries!"

"And bunyips," Ty smiles.

"Bloody bunyips!" Andy smiles back. "They get into everything."

"You're confusing bunyips with yowies," Ty says. "They're the real culprits."

"Ahhh, I see," Andy laughs.

They're becoming friends, I think. But then, maybe they're like me, nervous about handling a corpse and chatting out of necessity.

Within five minutes the roadway is clear and Nic drives the wagon closer to where the body lies. He jumps down and walks to the back of the wagon and slides out the tray that makes loading and unloading easier.

Andy helps Nic unfold a tarpaulin and lays it alongside the figure at our feet.

Then Nic leans down and gently rolls him over.

Early twenties. Perhaps Indian or Pakistani. Eyelids painted blue.

"There's no rigor mortis," Andy says softly.

"Delayed by cold water," Nic says.

Nic slides the young man's wallet out and flaps it open. A sodden Sleaze Ball ticket falls to the ground.

Ty retrieves it and hands it back like it's evidence. "Should we say a prayer?" he says.

"We don't know his beliefs," Nic says, "and don't want to insult him."

I remember the words Lana spoke at the base of the Bondi cliffs, and then again for Donut on the windowsill. "I've got something."

They look at me expectantly.

"Now we lay you down to sleep, we pray your Lord your soul to keep. If you should die before you wake, pray your Lord your soul to take."

Andy sighs, "Poor lad. Wrong place, wrong time."

"On the count of three," Nic says. "One. Two. Three." We lift the dead body and place him on the tarp. He's heavy. Nic folds and wraps the tarp gently over him and we carry him to the back of the wagon.

"Feet first," Nic says. "That way the body can't look back and beckon us to follow."

Engines sound loud and fast. Headlights turn down Riley from Oxford. A jeep accompanied by four bikes stops at the top of the rise.

Nic slides the body into the wagon. "I do the talking," he says.

The motorised group accelerates.

I pick up the bell and hold its tongue.

The jeep stops but the bikes weave noisily about and between us like they're replicating something from a movie. The horses spook but Nic manages to settle them.

"Easy! Easy!"

Engines cut. Headlights remain on.

"P plates," Andy says quietly. "They're just kids."

He's right. The jeep and all of the bikes have P plates.

The bikers remove their helmets to reveal white-painted faces, the hollows shaded to look like skulls.

In the jeep, behind the driver and the girl in the passenger seat, another white-face stands aiming the vehicle's fixed machine gun.

The driver lifts a radio receiver to his mouth.

"Unidentified vehicle located," he says. "Corner of Riley and Goulburn. Confirming it's the funeral carriage. Over."

He replaces the mouthpiece, gets out, and walks to the back of the wagon. He pulls the pistol strapped to his waist from its holster. It's Bondi, now graduated from bikes on the Bondi pathways to a jeep in the Hygiene Army. I retreat into more shadow.

Bondi lifts open the tarp covering the young man's face with the gun barrel. "Where are you going with this stiff?"

"Kinselas funeral parlour," Nic says. "We're picking up the bodies."

"By whose permission?" Bondi says.

"Civilised society," Nic says.

Bondi looks long and hard at Nic, then casually glances back at the girl in the jeep to make sure she is watching.

The goons slide off their bikes.

"But you're not civilised society, are you?" Bondi says. "You're just a bunch of filthy fags."

"If you insist," Nic says.

"I do insist, and I want you to repeat it," Bondi smirks. "What are you?"

Nic sighs, "Filthy fags."

"Now all of you," Bondi says.

"Filthy fags." Ty and I repeat.

"You." Bondi points to Andy who has kept his mouth closed. "Say it."

"I draw the line at 'filthy'," Andy says slowly.

"Just say it, Andy," Nic pleads from his seat upon the cart.

"Do I look filthy to you?" Andy says.

"I draw the line!" Bondi screeches.

There's a deafening crack. A bullet slams Andy against the side of the wagon. He slides to the ground.

My mind closes in on itself under the weight of the insanity. My bladder empties.

Bondi holsters his weapon and walks back to the vehicle. The shocked girl wears a crooked smile.

"There's another body you can pick up," Bondi yells. "Don't stop till you've carted away every filthy corpse!" He climbs back into the jeep, wrenches it into gear and accelerates away up the street. The bikers straddle their bikes and follow.

Andy is pulling in frantic breaths. Nic jumps down from the cart and gathers him in his arms. Ty and I crouch on either side. Helplessly we watch Andy gasp and start to spasm. Blood froths from his mouth. Incomprehension floods his eyes.

"No, no, no, no, no!" Nic beseeches as the rain drives down harder. I see the Grim Reaper approach. I close my eyes and bow my head.

.5.

We take the bodies back to Kinselas in the wagon and store them in the fridge. Then we return to the Burdekin. Nic goes up to tell Raft, and Ty and I tell Johnnie. Poor Johnnie is bereft. Ty and I are exhausted and just sit there.

Later we hear noises outside and find Nic collapsed against the wheel of the wagon sobbing his heart out. Raft has accused him of Andy's death, and says he never wanted to see him again. As Nic leads the horses away all manner of items come sailing down into the roadway smashing into smithereens. We race up to find Raft destroying the apartment, screaming to be left alone.

It takes two weeks to get official permission for the burial site and to prepare the ground. The cemetery is located in the building site for the new police station. The soil is soft after the rain, but it still takes two days to dig a trench long enough. My hands are blistered. Funnel web spiders are everywhere under the broken bits of masonry and brick. They emerge with their hairy front legs raised and fangs poised. Nic refuses to kill them, saying they can't help what they are.

Raft couldn't attend the mass burial because he was terrified of being recognised so we organised a private viewing for him in the cellar. Nic brought Andy's body back in the wagon and Ty, Johnnie and I, laid him on the pushed together tables where we'd sat around at dinner. Poor Nic had to wait outside while Raft said his goodbyes.

Coffins are assembled from the cemetery site's plywood hoarding. The same hoarding Andy commented on before his murder. 'Bill Posters' has now become code for our captors, because one day *he* will be prosecuted.

There's a number of women in the Grid. Dykes on Bikes without their wheels. Most entered on Sleaze Ball night in man drag. When asked why, one said, "to keep an eye on my gay brothers", which I thought meant she had actual gay brothers, but no, she meant her community. These women are the coffin builders and do a beautiful job with the tools at hand.

Big Red is in here, too. Her reasons are less altruistic. She told Nic, she hid during the forced evacuation because her property empire is within the wall's parameter and she wants to protect her holdings.

The saddest scene at the mass burial is the line of patients in the Koala Hotel's complimentary wheelchairs gazing into the trench, knowing they're likely to be next. Andy's body is lowered in first, then the student's, then the others. Twenty-three in all. Words are spoken but nothing diminishes anyone's pain. The only light moment is Frenchie squealing like a stuck pig after he disturbs a funnel-web with his shoe.

.6.

I am the scribe. It becomes my job to write the names in the Dead Book. My handwriting follows on from Andy's. He wrote the first name – the student's – and then his, in my hand, became the second. I've been writing their names ever since.

The walled enclosure is officially called Grid after the gay plague's first official moniker: Gay Related Immune Deficiency. So no one can forget what put us here. Posters detailing what we Must and Must Not Do are glued to the light poles and hoardings all up the street.

GRID RULES

ONE: Keep at least TWO METRES from the wall – DO NOT APPROACH THE WALL. Failure to comply may lead to injury, or death.

TWO: Obey ALL COMMANDS from Hygiene Party personnel. Failure to comply may lead to injury, or death.

THREE: DO NOT SPEAK to Hygiene Party personnel unless spoken to. Failure to comply may lead to injury, or death.

FOUR: OBEY CURFEW. Streets are to be clear of all human activity by 10pm. Failure to comply may lead to injury, or death.

FIVE: ANY attempt at escape may lead to injury, or death.

SIX: Rules may be added or modified AT ANY TIME. The onus is you to keep up-to-date. Failure to do so may lead to injury, or death.

*

The Emergency Response Committee, or the ERC, is in charge of the inner running. They run the hospital and soup kitchen, clean the streets, and find housing and supplies for new internees transported in on the plague buses that are filled with people identified by callers to the 'Dob a Deviant' hotline. The plague buses are government requisitioned interstate buses that many of us once caught voluntarily to this city.

The soup kitchen has four nightly sittings and is run by a drag queen and ex-navy cook named Betty. Johnnie works there chopping up vegetables, his handicap makes him unsuitable for lifting dead bodies.

Most of my days are spent keeping the cemetery tidy and digging trenches with Nic and Ty. We try to have one ready so it's not a mad rush when the bodies come *en masse*. Nic makes a habit of steering the cart round the perimeter of the wall to monitor any changes. Most guards retreat when we draw near and some even cross themselves. Nic says instilling fear is our only weapon.

The wall is primarily made up of high smooth cement panels approximately eleven feet high. Each panel carries the Gatt stamp in the middle of it. I feel shame I ever served that freak family.

There's no way out except through the fortified gates at Taylor Square, Whitlam Square, where Crown Street intersects with Campbell, and at Stanley. Unless I'm in the cart I give the entry and exit points wide berth. Bored guards are dangerous. They've have been known to force passing internees to dance until they drop and beat the ones that don't put enough effort into their own degradation.

At night searchlights rake the streets searching for curfew breakers. Punishment is swift. Next day a body will be waiting for us. I feel numb and constantly on edge. Equal parts. Shaken and strained. Served on ice.

A detail of the wall is that it bisects at the top creating a channel like the letter Y. Nic thinks it's a track for something we haven't seen yet.

When the Opera Lady cries on the other side a sudden wind rises up flinging rubbish and dust all along the roadway as if in response.

.7.

It's hard to believe this is the city of my childhood dreams, but the evidence is staring me in the face. Giant red letters have been fixed to the top of Centrepoint Tower like a corrupting crown. HYGIENE is literally the first and last thing touched by the sun's rays. At night it's lit up like the Hollywood sign.

Information not shown on television, or heard on the radio, comes in on the plague buses. It's through the disembarked we learn what happened to the women at the party once the men were funnelled into the Grid. They've been fitted with ankle monitors, and must attend re-education, as well as report weekly to the police. Apparently, lesbians are a conundrum for the government because the disease so far has left them alone making them harder to paint with the debauched brush, through no want of Bill Posters trying.

No one knows what happened to the Sisters of Perpetual Indulgence. The last sighting was when they were being herded onto a truck outside Sleaze Ball. A rumour is spreading that they were bundled onto a plane, flown out to sea, and flung out.

The claustrophobia gets worse in here each day. Every time the Opera Lady cries the air inside the walls heaves in her direction. It's the ghosts scrambling to reach her. The Opera Lady is their only escape and now she can't gain access to release them.

Bill Posters sets up a platform just inside the Taylor Square gate. Twice a week a bureaucrat in white face paint, sits at a table beneath a shade cloth and takes aid applications from the ERC. Five minutes at the end is reserved for a Freedom Plea. A lottery is drawn, and the winner gets the right to plead his case. It's mainly the closet cases who apply. The ones who lived double lives with wives and children. These men are naively hopeful they'll be able to convince Bill Posters there's been a terrible injustice. No one has been freed yet, and no one ever will. It's a sadistic form of entertainment for Bill Posters but it also reaps dividends when these poor suckers name names and betray those who live the same kind of lives but who, so far, have gone undetected.

These betrayals alert Nic to the danger facing Raft and he makes a strategic decision.

He informs Big Red that Raft has died and been buried in one of the mass graves. He does this so word will reach the Pied Piper and Frenchie and nix any ideas they may have gotten about using his existence as a bargaining chip. Nic even gets me to write Raft's name in the Dead Book as an extra precaution. Nic still protects Raft even though Raft refuses to talk to him.

Food and medicine are in short supply, but there's always music. Someone plays a record through an open window, another strums a guitar, another internee belts out opera on a street corner. It's soul food and if Bill Posters realised how important it was for our survival, he'd ban it. There are other entertainments but they're fleeting and impromptu. Drag acts and performance artists appear with no notice on the awnings and disappear just as quickly when Bill Posters sends in his goons to apprehend the 'troublemakers'. Street life empties at the first sound of the jeeps.

The Grid is being extended. The old decommissioned Darlinghurst Gaol is being connected with an enclosed tunnel. Hopefully it's extra accommodation as we're rapidly filling up.

Cyril Westacott is screaming blue murder. Someone climbed into his backyard and stole his last chicken. He's out roaming the streets smelling the air for cooking. God help the thief if he's caught.

Every pimple or blemish feels like a Kaposi sarcoma about to erupt.

.8.

Two main tribes evolve in the Grid – the Proboscis tribe (or the Pro-bites), and the Anti-bites (bug sluts). The Proboscis, the lesser-numbered tribe, follow the official line that the plague can be carried by mosquitoes. The Proboscis wear Bill Posters' repellent paint but dye it and cover their entire bodies with it. Over this they drape floor-length mozzie netting from intricate wire headdresses and helmets. Some even wear long, red, knitted sock-like appendages from their chins in honour of their name.

We call it disease drag. I can't take my eyes off them when they promenade slowly up and down the street, wielding long silver nozzles and poison packs squirting chemicals into every little hole and crevice to obliterate insect larvae. They've even a ritual dance full of strange bows and slow undulations that's performed when Proboscis meets Proboscis. It's like watching something from the height of the New Romantic movement except this fashion is led by fear, not freedom. Ty says it's like watching brolgas dance.

The Anti-bites are led by an entomologist who preaches his science on a milkcrate smack bang in the middle of Oxford and Crown. He's the same guy who was screeching the day of my job interview. He claims the government has known for a long time that the virus isn't mosquito borne, but the lie serves a purpose in that it keeps the general population under control. People now take him seriously. He's the one who christened the Pro-bites the Proboscis.

Johnnie, Ty, Nic, and me are Anti-bites. We're in the majority. The Proboscises call us bug sluts. Despite the name-calling most people get on. It's hard enough in here as it is.

The Burdekin Hotel cellar is now empty. A lot of the alcohol Johnnie had to barter for Raft's medicine and foodstuffs, but a lot also went down our gullets. Last night we polished off the last bottle with a cocktail-making competition. Bitter old Fernet-Branca – the drink no customer ever ordered – was the last bottle standing.

The winning cocktail was Johnnie's version of the tequila Lick-Sip-Suck. (Not technically a cocktail but beggars can't be choosers.)

'Spit on Bill's Grave' recipe:

A lick of ground black pepper.

Throw back 30 mls of Fernet-Branca.

Suck on the bottle of Worcestershire Sauce that Nic used for Bloody Marys.

The spit comes naturally.

.9.

Dinner and a show. Four times a night Betty the cook shimmies out from the kitchen and does a show – same song each sitting. Usually disco, always stupid, and designed to raise our spirits and to make up for the lack of food on our plates. God help anyone who just wants to watch *Neighbours* on the soup kitchen televisions.

Tonight, Betty had to cancel because of a televised prime ministerial announcement about the Grid, hosted by Australia's favourite television reporter, Ossie Austin. Betty intends to give commentary though. "Maybe they've found a cure," she muses into the microphone, "and I'll be the first to say hallelujah."

"Good evening," Ossie says on the screen. "I'm coming to you live from a secure facility in Western Sydney. With me is the Prime Minister and leader of the Hygiene Party. Welcome Prime Minister."

Betty hisses like a cat.

The Prime Minister attempts to look caring but nothing can hide the poisonous look in his snake eyes.

"Thanks Ossie," he says. "As you all know there's been a complete news blackout on anything to do with Grid. This has been necessary for security reasons, but the situation has now changed and it's time to bring the Australian public up to speed because WE are under attack."

Everyone stops eating their meagre portion.

The PM talks about morality. He talks about depravity. He speaks all the same words we've heard for years now. It's the never-ending story: our kind will always be blamed for everything bad that happens.

"This is why I ignore politics," I whisper to Ty. He nods but keeps his eyes on the Prime Minister as he explains why a wall had to be built.

"But the wall is not enough," the PM continues. "There are forces both inside and outside Grid that threaten us, and we must do everything in our power to counteract their plans. Already our security personal have had to deal with infected matter, human waste, including faecal – yes you heard correctly – being flung at them by those that inhabit Grid." He pauses to let the weight of that sink in. "But that's not the only threat to our health and wellbeing. Outside groups are aligning to destroy the wall."

"We're not alone!" Betty claps her hands in delight.

"Consequently, we've had to invest heavily in new surveillance equipment – brand new Australian technology called Boundary Riders, to which you are about to be introduced."

I remembered Nic's hypothesis about the channel at the top of the wall.

"Now Ossie," the Prime Minister says. "If I may, I must leave you to continue with the presentation."

"Of course, Prime Minister!" "You've got a country to run!"

"It's not that," the Prime Minister grins. "My wife likes me home for dinner by eight or else I'm in the doghouse."

Ossie laughs and shakes his head.

The Prime Minister's car, glittering with raindrops, drives into the facility leaving wet tyre marks behind it. The camera films him sliding into the back seat.

"Give me a fucken break, this is all bullshit!" Betty gestures at the soup kitchen's windows. "It's not raining outside. The weather report said clear skies. This isn't live. This was filmed during that downpour we had months ago… No one's flung shit at anyone. This is all staged."

Betty's right.

"The Prime Minister has mentioned them already so let me introduce you to a Boundary Rider," Ossie says. "Bring on Blue!"

"Fasten your seatbelts everybody!" Betty says. There is a drum-roll as the camera rotates to reveal a mock-up of the Grid wall sticking out through long red velvet curtains.

A large metallic blue ball fifteen times the size of an inflatable beachball, rolls out on the track. A technician appears alongside carrying a clip board.

Ossie pumps the tech's hand. "This magnificent machine must be Blue."

"Correct," the tech says.

"How many Boundary Riders are there?"

"We're aiming for a fleet of ten for the Sydney Grid," the tech says. "Once they are proven, there will be many more."

"And this technology is Aussie made?"

"100 percent," the tech says proudly. "The export market will be huge. The entire world is crying out for Boundary Riders."

"And we're the guinea pigs!" Betty exclaims.

"Now is it true they come in different colours?" Ossie is saying.

"Yes," the tech says. "They need individual signifiers to help with identification, but the colours are interchangeable to confuse the enemy."

"Can Blue see and hear?" Ossie says.

"Sure can." The tech begins ticking off his fingers. "Blue's got top of the line infrared vision that can zoom in faster and further than a hawk's eye, even through smoke, and its hearing abilities are finer than a Doberman's."

Ossie pats Blue's panelled side. "Self-controlled?"

"Not yet," the tech says. "For now, each Boundary Rider has a team of expert controllers and Grid will be individually managed 24/7 from Centrepoint Tower."

I feel shocked that the beacon that drew me here has been corrupted this way. First the crown of letters and now this.

"Now mate," Ossie says, "You've got some footage to show us how fast these babies can move." He rubs his hands together. "So, let's settle back and watch a display of Blue's capabilities."

Like giant bowling balls the Boundary Riders race along a winding track. They're beautiful and mesmerising, moving so quick they blur. They pull into sidings built into the wall to allow each other passage. 'To enable the machine best suited to the emergency,' the voiceover explains.

"I wouldn't like to be chased by one of those bad boys," Ossie says.

"Don't do anything deviant," the tech grins, "and you won't be."

"That's not hard, is it? Don't be deviant, people!" Ossie guffaws as other technicians enter carrying a life-sized, wooden cut-out figure of a man covered in purple spots.

Eyes wide we gape at one another. Shouts of laughter fill the soup kitchen. "Is that meant to represent us?" Betty yells.

"Who's this?" Ossie says.

"This sick character is an infected Griddite attempting to escape so he can spread the gay plague to the outside world."

Ossie pretends alarm. "What can Blue do to stop this dangerous criminal?"

"What do you think shoots from Blue?" the tech asks.

"Pepper spray?" Ossie proposes. "Hot water?"

"It's hot alright." The tech hands Ossie protective headgear and leads him behind a transparent body shield.

"First," the tech says, "the Boundary Rider will start flashing to warn the spreader he's got time to reconsider his actions."

Blue starts flashing. Colours of all kind roil through its skin like the aurora borealis on fast forward.

"Then the Boundary Rider will turn black to alert the spreader its weapon is about to discharge."

Blue turns jet black like a black hole opening up.

"Then the ball will fire."

A sharp blue flash. An explosion. Both Ossie and the tech duck their heads. The smoke settles to reveal the figure's legs are all that remains. Everything above mid-thigh has been obliterated.

We're agog.

"What's that word?" Ossie says, pulling off his ear protection and shaking his head. "Smiting! That's it. Like the finger of God!"

We stare dully at the usual advertisements: Grim Reaper, one for the Hygiene Party, one for the Dob in a Deviant Hotline, and a new one, one aimed at children: "Boundary Riders! Collect all ten! Enter the competition to name each one! Win a trip to their top-secret facility and meet them all. In newsagents now! Wall and track pieces sold separately."

When Betty finally flicks the TV off, Ty says, "We're doomed."

.10.

Johnnie confesses to us that he stole Cyril's chicken to feed Raft. He's also been giving Raft his hard-boiled egg and denying his own body sustenance.

Johnnie's loyalty to Raft goes back to the days when Johnnie was first saved by Andy and he's remained loyal to a 'T', although it should be an 'A' for Andy. Johnnie's even been stealing from the soup kitchen fridges.

Food theft in the Grid is a killing matter. Ty, Nic, and I know because we've dealt with the bodies. We decide unanimously not to tell Cyril what happened to his chook.

Johnnie stealing for Raft is the final straw for Nic. Johnnie is now a pigeon catcher. Nic taught him how to set snares in the hotel's second and third floors where the birds have gained access to shelter from the weather. The halt in renovations has left gaps and holes all over the place. Nic learnt how to set snares in prison where the prisoners kept the birds as pets. Now Johnnie supplies meat for the hospital, and as payment for the birds, brings home cooked squab that he gives to Raft. Johnnie now also gets to eat his own eggs.

Every day, Ty, Nic, and I cart bodies and dig holes and once done I come home and flop in the bed I've made in the shell of Andy's dismantled car, resting on bricks in the garage. It's too cramped upstairs to share Johnnie's space. I want to find a bigger place for the three of us, but Johnnie won't leave Raft, and Ty won't leave Johnnie, and I can't leave either of them. It's comfortable enough, and if the goons discover the car body, they won't bother removing it because they'll think it's a wreck. That's my assumption anyway.

I'm not sure if Ty and Johnnie are back together. I'm not sure if they know either.

The Opera Lady cries from the other side of the wall. The wind that follows slams doors and sends paper and dirt flying. The ghosts are getting angry.

A news report on the soup kitchen's television shows a huge blaze in

Brisbane which, the newsreader says, is the Brisbane Grid on fire. This is the first we'd heard of other Grids in other cities. It looks like the whole of Fortitude Valley is up in flames. I wonder about the Terminus. The newsreader explains that it's an industrial fire that's gotten out of control. The cameras aren't allowed too close.

.11.

The Boundary Riders – Bill Posters' bowling balls – arrive in all their shiny candy coloured glory. All the colours of the rainbow and more. Crowds of us stand in the street watching them roll along their groove as the technicians begin trialling each one on their home track.

I am reminded of the bottles in the Gold Bar all lined up like exotic birds in an aviary and I change the Boundary Riders' names. Red is Campari, yellow is Galliano, green is Crème de Menthe, black is Sambuca, purple is Parfait Amour, blue is Curaçao, brown is Whisky, orange is Grand Marnier, white is Ouzo, pink is Framboise.

At night they make a high-pitched whine as they zoom along the wall track and all the lights in the Grid flicker when they accelerate to optimum speed. I know they're Bill Posters' bowling balls, but I'm excited to see them even if they are portents of our doom. There's nothing much else to get excited about. Exhaustion and hunger make us all lethargic. If we're not working, or sleeping, we're sitting zoned out on the street watching our enclosed world go by.

Watching Galliano and Parfait Amour play speed tag I hear Big Red tell Nic that with all the dirt she knows about everybody 'running this shit show' it's safer for her inside the Grid than out. That her house is her castle and it's impenetrable. That when the goons came calling on the night the wall went up they failed to gain access, despite using a battering ram.

I hear Nic ask how she handles the Pied Piper and Frenchie who've been noticeably quiet and well-behaved since the wall went up.

"Don't you worry," she says. "That pair won't say boo with what I know. I've got them on very short leads."

"You must have some powerful dirt on them to keep them quiet," Nic says.

"Niccy boy, the dirt I've got on that pair is dynamite."

I wonder if what she knows about them is the same that Bambi knew. Before he used my box-cutter to slit his own throat.

.12.

The Innocents are men, women, and children infected via contaminated blood supplies through no fault of their own. They inhabit the old Darlo gaol – now called the Lazaret – and access the Grid through the new tunnel.

We knew they were coming due to the new Grid rule number six: You must BOW if an Innocent walks within two metres, but under NO circumstances are you allowed to communicate in any other way. Failure to comply may lead to injury, or death.

They wear white monk-like robes and the Pro-bites among them paint their faces and hands in the same white paint as the Hygiene Army, despite the fact they're already infected. It's a noble act. They paint themselves to stop mosquitoes drawing their blood and transferring the infection onto others. The painted ones look like angels without wings, and that's the idea.

Innocents get better food, medical care, and are free from contributing manpower to the work details. They've a self-ordained leader; a religious nutter named Hank – the same guy who used to scream on his milk crate about mosquitoes and Jesus in the pre-wall days, in direct opposition to the entomologist on his crate. One of the very few things that's like the old days.

Now though, Hank's thundering list of the mosquito borne diseases – malaria, dengue, yellow fever, encephalitis – trumps the entomologist screeching difficult science about a mosquito proboscis being nothing like a hypodermic syringe, when, to the uneducated and gullible, that's exactly what a proboscis looks like.

Rule number six allows Hank to attack the entomologist, but the entomologist is forbidden direct reply. The entomologist, in his frustration, is his own worst enemy. He labels the crowd 'idiots' and 'half-wits' which pushes the confused into the arms of the other camp. It's a sad spectacle, but these days any spectacle is a good spectacle.

Bill Posters has ordered bonfires to burn 24/7 on every second street corner for the smoke to repel insects. Nic thinks the true purpose of the fires is to test the capability of the Boundary Riders' infrared technology to penetrate the smoke. As Betty says, "we're nothing but guinea pigs."

Smoke, Boundary Riders, preachers screaming, the weirdly dressed, makes the street appear both space age and medieval.

*

Grid workers receive a small stipend of one hard-boiled egg every second day, but there's a rumour it's to be reduced to one a week. Up till now Ty's been giving his egg to an ancient Aboriginal man who'd been bused in from Woop Woop and who sits huddled in one of the Oxford Street door-ways. I halve mine with Ty. He brings the salt and pours it into the palm of his hand. We eat it sitting on the footpath with our feet in the gutter and talk about the days when we used to share the leftovers from the foot-ball ground kiosk.

I worry Ty will continue expecting me to share my egg with him if the allowance is reduced.

Johnnie is finding birds hard to come by so he can't be relied upon to feed us and Raft. It was a good idea of Nic's, but Johnnie's snares are often empty. No one knows where the birds have gone.

.13.

I'm sitting on the front step of Zink & Sons, listening to an internee singing on my old scabbing corner when Connor, the ex-chef from the Dining
Room, comes walking down Oxford Street with his Innocent hood pushed
back revealing his thick brown hair and hazel eyes. Despite his severe weight
loss and facial lesions, I recognise him immediately. He always had the
kindest eyes. He is not wearing face paint, so I know he's Anti-bite. He
recognises me too and stops then pretends to read the latest Grid announcement dictating that everyone in the Grid, (minus the Innocents) must
submit to a blood test.

As dictated by law I stand and bow then step back into Zink's entryway
to make myself less noticeable. Rule number six makes it illegal for us to
speak, so we use sly hand signals to communicate. I mime being hungry
more as a joke about how he used to hide desserts for me in exchange for
stronger staff drinks. He mimes being drunk and pretends sadness when I
hold up empty hands to say no more drinks.

He makes it known I'm to be back in this spot in two days' time.

*

Collecting the dead is a curse. The living steer clear of us even when we're
off-duty. Nic says if he'd known of this outcome, he'd have made us wear
masks like old-time executioners. He suggests we dilute the impression we're
the Grim Reaper's minions by performing other work on the side. He has
Cyril Westacott to help him with the lighter duties and can afford to cut
us some slack. Nic and Cyril get on like a house on fire.

Nic pulls strings with Eddy at the ERC, and so now Ty and I have two
jobs. First, carting/boxing/burying bodies, and second, working at the

Oxford Processing Centre (the old Oxford Hotel public bar).

My primary role at the OPC is to fill in the Living Book after new intern-ees step down off the plague buses that roll in through the Taylor Square gate. The Living Book isn't the official name but that's what I call it. Writing living names counterbalances writing dead names and feels like a reprieve.

Ty's job is to find billets for the new inhabitants by scouring the accom-modation map. The Grid is rapidly running out of space, even the cemetery. The Innocents cremate their own dead and smoke winds up out of the Laza-ret's tall chimney and settles over the Grid. Smells like bacon.

Death goes on all around. Some men hang from roof beams. Some over-dose in their baths. Some step off building ledges. Some chose the needle, or gas. The bell rings and rings and rings. *So long, so long, so long.*

.14.

I'm teaching Johnnie and Ty how to scab cigarettes on the Yurong Street stairs when I hear the sounds of singing echoing through the gaps in the buildings.

Click! Click! Click!

"What's that?" Ty says.

"Click Go the Shears?" Johnnie says.

The gates at the Whitlam Square open and a column of bedraggled men file in.

Click Go the Queers, Boys, Click! Click! Click!

Leading them is Destiny, from the Terminus nightclub in Brisbane. A wide-eyed blond boy runs behind her like a lamb after its mother. Destiny has a bruised face but otherwise looks uninjured. Representatives from the ERC rush down and siphon off the wounded to the hospital. The rest are directed to the Processing Centre.

Ty and I race up the street to man our posts.

Destiny and her young shell-shocked protégé are the first in. Destiny nudges the blond forward.

"Do this one first," Destiny directs me.

"Name?" I ask the boy gently.

"Crystal Night," Destiny says before he can utter a word. "My most divine creation."

"Last home address?"

"Just write the Terminus," Destiny says.

"Occupation?"

"She's a fucking star!"

I turn the page.

"Now you," I tell Destiny.

"You know who I am," Destiny says. "Just write everything else same as hers."

They move on to Ty. Destiny leans over the counter and forces a hug on him. "Well if it ain't Aboriginal Abigail! I knew you'd end up behind bars!"

"Get off me," Ty laughs. "You stink as much as your jokes."

"*Eau de Manure.*" Destiny batts her lashes. "We're all wearing it in Brisbane these days. It's the latest thing."

Her eyes fill with tears as she whispers starkly, "They kept us in cattle cars. Two hundred of us. We've been through hell and back. We lost six on the train and God knows how many back in the riot."

"There was a riot?" Ty says.

"Oh, darling! We rose up!" Destiny says proudly. "We set the whole fucking place on fire! That's why we're here. They had nowhere else to put us."

.15.

Beautiful Connor drops a crème caramel in my hands as he walks past the Zink & Sons alcove. I could devour it right there. No one would know. Instead I run back to the garage where there is just enough for Nic, Ty, Johnnie and me to have two small teaspoons each. The first spoon tastes like walls collapsing, birds singing, and flowers blooming. The second makes us weep.

Food is basic and the meals get smaller every week. Meat is now literally non-existent. Johnnie hasn't caught a bird for ages and Nic is sleeping with the horses in case people start dreaming of Psychopomp pie.

Internees barter whatever they can get their hands on for the things they can't. Food, alcohol, cigarettes are top of the list, then medicine. The hospital pharmacy is running on empty. Vitamins and minerals are in high demand as people swallow and inject anything in the hope of staying alive. Rumour and falsehood run rife. Charlatans fill the void by peddling all manner of snake oil as plague cures. Stalls at the ghetto market sell unguents and elixirs made from bones, shit, powdered insects and urine.

Nasturtium leaves are an accepted currency.

*

Blood results are back. Negatives must now wear green collars. Positives wear red.

Nic's collar is red. So's Johnnie's. So's Ty's.

Mine's green.

I'm the odd man out and I don't know how to feel. The relief feels obscene.

.16.

I am stretching my legs having just processed a plague bus from the Central Coast when the Opera Lady's cry emanates from the other side of the wall. It has that high keening quality of a cat separated from her kittens. Again, the wind comes howling. Two proboscises stop their promenade and turn to the wall to shield their faces from the dust.

The empty plague bus is still parked outside the centre. The driver is in his seat eating lunch and writing in his logbook. He closes the driver-side window against the dirt and grit but leaves the vehicle's middle doors open to air the stench of unwashed bodies from the vehicle. An internee, one of the new ones, slides along the side of the bus clutching a screwdriver. I'm too surprised to do or say anything. He sneaks aboard, races up the middle, and presses the tip against the driver's neck. He forces the driver to start the engine and then flings him out onto the footpath. Two other internees jump aboard whooping as the bus reverses down the street.

The ejected driver scrambles for the gate. He runs yelling but the tower guards don't recognise him or understand what he is screaming. They open fire. Bullets ricochet and I take cover in a doorway as two Boundary Riders – Campari and Curaçao – roll in on the wall track. The bus reverses to Crown Street and then accelerates straight back towards Taylor Square. Campari begins flashing then turns black. The internee has no time to change his mind.

Flames roar. The bus explodes and careens into the gateway. A wave of intense heat forces me into the nearest sheltered doorway where I drop to the ground. I peer out through all the smoke and dust. The two proboscises have become shrieking torches. The vehicle, now a burning wreck, has created a hole, and there, picking her way through in all her pristine glory, is the Opera Lady.

Somehow, she makes it through and releases three calls in quick succession. The heat and smoke roil up, as if under her command, pulling all the dust and bits of debris into a rotating funnel. The ghosts of the Grid surge into it. The wind is incredible. Scrambling to my feet I see, in the strange carnivalesque lights bouncing off the dust particles, ascending cages of a Ferris wheel full of joyous souls. Andy is one of them. He looks beatific.

The Opera Lady's satin slippers are arrow heads and continue their sharp aim down the street.

As the old Indigenous man abandons his doorway and walks towards her, arms outstretched, blue Curaçao starts flashing like the aurora borealis.

People hang from windows calling, "Don't shoot! Don't shoot!"

The old man and the Opera Lady meet in the middle. They bow to one another and as their heads touch, an obliterating flash claims them.

The shockwave causes the awning above me to collapse and I am trapped behind it as screaming internees lose their minds and rush the gate. The Ferris wheel dissolves. I hear goons shooting and flashes discharging from the Boundary Riders. I curl into a ball.

Under the gaze of Bill Posters we bury what little is left of the Opera Lady and the old man amongst the palm trees on Gilligan's Island. The rest of the casualties including the careless bus driver and the proboscises, wait their turn in Kinselas.

.17.

On our hundredth night a candlelight rally is held to honour our dead. Beginning at the cemetery, a thousand of us walk slowly up Crown, down Liverpool, up the Yurong Street stairs, cross Oxford, down Pelican, and back to the cemetery. A hushed golden river, as if the turret of Centrepoint has melted and flowed into the Grid.

Afterwards, Ty and I see Frenchie, Pied Piper, and his blond twins, wandering about the graves. Perhaps they're paying their respects but that seems far-fetched.

Raft still hasn't come downstairs and Johnnie must source all his needs. Neither Ty nor I are allowed to help. Raft blames us as well as Nic for being present at Andy's death and doing nothing to stop it.

I want to scream, "Blame the cufflinks. Don't blame us!"

*

The entomologist's corpse is found in a back lane. He's been run over by a truck. His death reeks of silencing. We keep our eyes down as we shovel his body into the wagon.

I will miss his screeching science, and now Hank's rantings will go completely unopposed.

Goons hooning = more street bashings. I remember thinking, in pre-wall days, that if one was built it would at least keep the street violence down. I failed to consider the goons building the wall. Now Bill Poster's goons invade the Grid bashing and robbing (except the Innocents) whenever they desire.

The Pro-bites have become a force to be reckoned with. Seduced by fear, more and more Anti-bites have switched sides and begun to paint their faces and don the mosquito net. A new fashion called Plague Wear has sprung up. Wire cutters and moulders, dyers, and mosquito net drapers all set up their stalls at the ghetto market and showcase their wares.

The Innocents have been quick adopters of these fashions, but only in white so as to keep themselves differentiated from the guilty. Business with them is done silently by hand movements and written instructions. Payment is made with food. Wind chimes and tiny bits of broken glass and mirror are used to ornament the Innocents' ensembles to give them extra pizzazz. Hank's outfit is the most elaborate. He has a team of sycophants to help him into his regalia. He moves slowly up and down Oxford Street like the Pope.

*

Big Red is in a coma. Spider bite. There's no anti-venom in the Grid. I remember the Pied Piper and Frenchie wandering about the cemetery with the blond twins 'paying their respects'. Ty tells me to keep my mouth shut or else I'll put a target on my back. It dawns on me that Bambi might not have taken his own life. Maybe another hand wielded the box-cutter.

.18.

Birds are now non-existent in the Grid. Even the fruit bats give the area a wide berth. No one knows why. Some blame the bonfire smoke, or the electromagnetics of the Boundary Riders. Johnnie now only catches rats and mice. Poor Raft thinks he's still eating pigeon. Johnnie hasn't the heart to tell him. Raft would die if he knew. Maybe he does. Maybe we're all dead and this is hell.

No sign of the Pied Piper or Frenchie at Big Red's funeral. Her corpse barely cold, they've taken over her house – the biggest in the Grid – and the ERC is powerless to stop it. There are rumours they're going to turn it into a brothel. Johnnie is terrified they're going to come for him. Nic says, "not over my dead body." Ty says, "they'll have to get through me first." I say, "ditto."

*

The Countess arrives with a knock on the garage door. Unbelievable. Everyone cries. She only has half an hour. Organised by Arno Gatt to spite his father she's come in disguised as one of the wall technicians. The Countess brings chocolate. Nic tells her about Andy. Shocked, she tells Nic their Da has died, broken by the forced evacuation and loss of home and livelihood.

Nic falls and the Countess catches him. He clings to her like a drowning sailor. I help her lower him into a chair. The Countess demands the cufflinks and asks if I've been consulting them.

I tell her about the night Andy was murdered and explain how the scarab cufflink seemed to suggest we were given permission to go out and retrieve the bodies.

"I would have read them the same way," she says, turning the lidded jar over and over in her hands. She unscrews the lid and pulls out the scarab again.

"Papa!" she hisses. "What does it mean?"

Nic opens his eyes, "Unfinished business."

His sister agrees.

Before leaving, the Countess tells us of the underground movement of activists working to bring down the wall and not to lose hope. Says she'll be back.

*

Ghosts hang from the Oxford Street awnings. Their feet brush against me like jelly fish, or the cold wet sleeves and trouser legs on a clothesline. The ghosts' focus is on elevation. It's a hunger to them. They're waiting for the Opera Lady to come and release them, but the Opera Lady has climbed aboard the Ferris wheel and flown away. The feeling of claustrophobia in the Grid has never been this bad. Makes me gulp for air.

I understand now the birds and bats give the Grid wide berth because they're sick of ghosts grabbing at them trying to hitch a ride.

Different types of spirits are trapped here. Each with their own energy. Those who have perished from the sickness are the most plentiful. A deep sadness overcomes me when I blunder into their hanging feet. The younger ones are the worst and leave a terrible itch. Even the slightest touch makes me come away feeling like the one-legged ballet dancer scratching his lost limb. The most bearable are the older ones who had the chance to experience something of life before succumbing. Their sadness drapes over me like a soft caul. Then there are those who couldn't wait for the fingers of the Grim Reaper to pluck them from the living crowd and have done it to themselves. They give me a constricted breathless feeling as if I'm wearing clothes three sizes too small. The ghosts of the murdered are red chip angry and give me the jitters.

When I'm writing ghosts hover round the car shell in which I lie, steering my pen and feeding me words. They refuse to be forgotten.

I know I'm not mad. I'm not the only one who senses these spirits. People are crying out on the street for no reason, or bursting into tears, or lashing out at nothing with their fists.

.19.

After my shift at the Oxford Processing Centre I return to the garage and see the door leading to the cellar open. I find Nic, Johnnie, and Ty sitting in the light of a flickering candle at Table One. They're naked to the waist, their chests and arms are glistening with gold stripes, dots, and dashes, they've been anointing one another with. Two bottles of black-market vodka sit empty before them. The gold dispenser lays dismantled. Their sense of intimacy stops me pulling up a chair. I lean against the bar.

"Ahem."

They turn their unfocused eyes upon me like meat-eaters high on blood. Gold glimmers about their mouths and glitters across their foreheads and cheeks. The candle throws their profiles against the tiled wall.

"Don't look at me like that," Ty rasps.

"Like what?" I say.

"Like I'm a hypocrite drinking gold."

"I'm not," I say. "I just wish I'd been invited."

"You don't need any." He lets loose a burp. "You're Negative."

"Where'd you find the gold?"

"Under the bar," Nic says. "It's the off-cuts I'd stashed and forgotten."

"What did you trade for the vodka?" I say, thinking the answer will be rat meat.

Johnnie raises his hand. "Me."

Nic lifts his glass. "If a job's worth doing it's worth doing well."

"Cheers!" The three of them drain their drinks.

Johnnie displays his patterned arms in the candlelight. "Guess what I am?"

"Drunk?" I say.

"A cheetah!"

Ty laughs and tips his glass at him.

"What are you?" I ask Ty.

"Black panther."

I look at Nic, "You?"

He shrugs.

Ty takes one of Nic's golden arms and Johnnie takes the other and they inspect each appendage like they're play-acting Howard Carter in Tutankhamun's tomb.

"He's a sphinx," Johnnie says.

Ty runs his tongue along Nic's forearm. "Tiger!"

Nic lets out a laugh as they fall upon him.

"I'll let the three of you get on with it," I say as they begin devouring one another.

*

The next day I wander back into the bar and survey the abandoned bottles and three empty glasses. I remember how the Countess would perform gold leaf readings for a select few. I pick up Nic's glass, then Johnnie's, then Ty's. I see the same sign encrusted in all three. I rush to the sink and wash them out. *So long. So long. So long...*

.20.

Bondi hoons through the streets with his crew extorting stallholders at the ghetto market, upending tables, bashing pedestrians and running amok.

"He thinks he can get away with murder. I wish I had something on him to show him justice comes in many forms." Nic's anger has percolated since his father died.

"Kit had a run in with him. Before the wall," Ty says.

Nic's eyes glitter as he stares at me.

"He and his gang were notorious for chasing gays off the Bondi cliffs," I say. "We pegged stones at him on the pathway. We were the ones that got away."

"Why haven't you mentioned this earlier?"

"It didn't seem important."

"Tell me now. Every little detail," Nic says.

*

Nic lets his stubble grow, paints dark circles under his eyes, and jams a low-brimmed hat on his head. He wraps his foot in dirty bandages, borrows one of Johnnie's crutches and practices carrying an injury.

"Hell's bells!" Johnnie exclaims. "Can you tone down the Quasimodo?"

"I used to work in the best bar in town and now I'm the body carter," Nic says, peering into the mirror above Johnnie's sink. "It's imperative to the mission that no one recognises me."

"You look completely different," I say. "And you've lost weight."

"Give me your green collar, Kit. I'll have better luck catching this fish if I'm wearing the colour of the Negative. He won't engage with me if he thinks I'm a Positive."

My heart skips a beat. Nic sees my reluctance to wear the red.

"Of course," I say, untacking it from my neck and handing it over. Putting his on makes me feel ill.

Nic sets up a stall in the furthest corner of the ghetto market and lays out all the Countess's cufflinks on black felt. Then he waits. His disguise is convincing and no one pays him much attention. Ty and I perform his regular body hauling duties but it's a quiet week and nothing we can't handle.

I pretend to browse while giving Nic an account of a body we've picked up when the sound of motorbikes fills the marketplace.

"Too late for a quick getaway," Nic says. "Get under the table."

I drop and hide. Through the folds in the tablecloth I see five of them – all white faced and armed. Bondi and the girl who was in the jeep the night Andy was murdered wander among the stalls as if they were on a date at the Paddington Markets in pre-wall times. The other three goons go about collecting payments and threatening.

The girl stops in front of Nic's stall. "Get a load of these," she says, indicating the cufflinks. "I might get you a set."

Bondi slaps her arse. "Only faggots wear jewellery."

"You're wearing a ring," she challenges.

"It's my grandfather's signet ring," he says. "That's different."

"Still jewellery," She says matter-of-factly, "and these gun cufflinks are cool." She looks at Nic. "How much?"

"On the house." Nic offers.

Bondi lunges over the table. "They're all on the house!" he seethes.

"You're right! They are!" Nic pretends to cower as the girl moves off to the next stall.

Bondi snarls, "I ain't seen you before. No one works here without paying me."

"I've just started." Nic whines. He drops his voice. "I don't have any money. But I have information."

"What information?" Bondi says.

"This guy I know brags about an incident between you and him on the Bondi pathway. He laughs about it all the time."

"What incident?"

"Some incident where he struck your little brother with stones and forced you to say something untrue."

Through Bondi's legs I see the other goons heading for the table. One calls, "Come on boss? What's taking you so long?"

"I'm teaching this fag what the deal is round here. Go wait for me at the bikes." Turning back to Nic, he hisses. "Forced me to say what?"

Nic waves the crutch he's borrowed from Johnnie. "Promise you won't shoot the crippled messenger?"

"I'll shoot you if you don't get hurry up and tell me," Bondi growls.

"He says he forced you to claim you're a faggot." Nic whispers. "So, I can't pay you, but I could find out where this guy lives?"

"Be here with the information in three days," Bondi says. "or your life won't be worth shit."

"My life's not worth shit already," Nic states blankly, "but it gives me pleasure to know that little braggart will get his just desserts. He treats me like dirt because I'm a cripple. All the young ones do."

"He won't for much longer," Bondi says as he turns away.

After the goons have departed, I crawl out from beneath the table.

"Are we going to kill him?" I say, counting the ways.

"I've killed one man and won't kill another," Nic says.

"So, what are we going to do with him then?"

"You'll see."

How do you know he'll take the bait?"

"He's already taken the bait," Nic says. "The question is whether he's paranoid enough to try and exact his revenge himself. The problem for him is that if he brings in his lackeys, they'll find out what the revenge is for. I need him to come in alone."

*

A little girl steps off the plague bus holding a doll. The paperwork handed to us by the driver indicates she is meant to go to the Lazaret.

Ty drops to his haunches. "That's a nice doll. What's her name?"

"George."

"That's an interesting name."

"She's a tomboy," the girl says, quietly.

Ty grabs at invisible branches. "Does she climb trees?"

The little girl nods.

Ty pretends to grab invisible creatures off the ground. "Catch lizards?"

Nod.

"Plays with train sets?"

Nods.

"Well, can I be George's friend, too?" Ty says.

Nod.

Ty gives the doll's hand a little shake. "Hello George. Pleased to meet you. My name is Ty. If you ever want to climb a tree, or catch a lizard, come find me okay?" Ty points to the girl, "You can bring your friend, but we should probably be introduced. What's her name?"

He leans in to hear the doll's answer.

He sits back in pretend dismay. "I know you said something, but I didn't catch it."

He cleans his ear with his finger and the little girl laughs.

It's pure sunshine. Her laugh blazes the fog away. We gaze at her in wonder. Ghosts bundle together and zoom.

"Nope," Ty says, smacking the side of his head. "Can't hear a thing. Must be deaf."

"Ivy!" the girl exclaims. "My name is Ivy!"

"Pleased to meet you, Ivy!" Ty extends his hand.

Alerted by the noise, a young man – one of the Innocents – hurries over. "Come away child, do not touch him."

"Why not!" Ty says. "What makes you think you're any different from us?"

The man takes the child's arm. "We are completely different. We're incarcerated because your kind polluted the blood supply. It's you that made her sick. Remember that, faggot."

*

Nic returns from the ghetto market and flings himself down on Johnnie's couch. We wait for his news.

"Bondi's swallowed the story hook, line, and sinker," he says. "He's coming in alone."

"How did you arrange that?" I slosh some black-market rum into a cup and hand it to him.

Nic grimaces at the taste. "I told him that I had a way to ensure you're comatose and no threat."

"Me?"

"Yep, you're bait. You just have to lie in Johnnie's bed and pretend to be in a drugged sleep."

"How will he access the garage?" Johnnie says.

"I told him I know how to pick locks."

"And he believed you?"

Nic shrugs. "He's blinded by his success rate and his idiot ego."

"What happens when he's in the garage?" Ty says.

"Chloroform," Nic says. "There's a bottle at Kinselas. Morticians use it in embalming fluid. We let Bondi get to Kit and then grab him."

"Na, too risky," Ty says. "You're putting Kit in danger and you're forgetting Johnnie and I are in on this. Between us we can incapacitate Bondi on the laneway stairs."

"That'll work," Nic says. "We'll just have to carry him to the garage."

"Then what?" Johnnie says.

"Then we take some incriminating photographs on this little baby," Nic says, pulling out a polaroid camera from his knapsack.

"Where did you get that?" I say.

"Ghetto market. It cost two hard boiled eggs."

Johnnie raises his cup. "For Andy!"

Raising mine, I add, "And for all those chased off the cliffs."

*

Nic leans on his crutch in the shadows at the head of the Liverpool Street stairs while Ty and I lurk behind the bins at the base. Johnnie hides further along in a hidden recess with the chloroform bottle. The whine of the hated Boundary Riders, a constant reminder that we're meant to be following curfew.

Ty stands up. "This doesn't feel right. Why would he risk coming along Oxford Street? Any Rider would be able to see him. Let's hide further down with Johnnie."

We've just settled into our new positions when Bondi, gun drawn, slides into the lane and checks behind the bins we've just left for a potential ambush. He's early and has come from a different direction than he said he would.

Satisfied there's no trap he whistles to attract Nic.

Nic masks his shock and swings down the stairs on his crutch. "There you are boss! You said you'd meet me at the top."

"You think I'm an idiot? I had to make sure you're acting alone."

"You've got to trust me, boss," Nic whines. "I wanna see you punish that little bitch."

"I don't give a damn what you want."

"That still won't diminish my pleasure," Nic says, "and, I just wanna say, if you ever need anything, any information, or anything done in here then I'm your man, right boss?"

"You talk too much," Bondi says. "Where the fuck is he?"

Nic sniggers. "He's comatose waiting just for you. Just down this lane and up a flight of stairs."

"Is there anybody else around?" Bondi says.

"Na," Nic says. "These lanes are empty. Mainly old garages and storage units. No one but the little braggart lives here."

"Lead the fucking way," Bondi growls.

"This way," Nic says. "Follow me, boss."

We hear a thwack and a grunt, followed by the metallic thud of Bondi's gun hitting the ground. We race up and find Nic, crutches discarded, straddling Bondi and pinning his arms against the small of his back. Ty and I weren't needed.

"Fucking fucks!" Bondi seethes. "I'm going to kill you!"

"Shut up," Nic says calmly. "Your luck's run dry."

"What are you going to do?"

"You'll see." Nic nods to Johnnie. Johnnie presses the chloroform rag against Bondi's nose and mouth. He struggles and falls limp. We carry his unconscious body into the garage and up the stairs. We strip him naked and lay him out on Johnnie's bed.

I light some candles, saying, "Let's make it romantic."

"Fuck romance." Johnnie unscrews the lid from an amyl nitrate bottle and places it on the bedside table. "Make sure you get the amyl in the picture. Devil's in the details."

Nic holds the camera. "I've only got sixteen shots, so make each one work."

"I'm the expert." Johnnie pulls off his clothes. "Let me go first."

"No," Ty says. "Every part of your body is too recognisable. Let Kit."

Nic takes ten close-ups of me rolling around Bondi bare-arsed. It's strange being naked in front of Nic. Nic stops between each shot and directs me to angle Bondi's face to make sure he's identifiable in each. Eyes closed Bondi looks in ecstasy.

The camera spits out the square images. Nic hands them to Ty who shakes them dry and lays them in a row on the couch.

"Exhibit one, two, and three, Your Honour." Ty stands back and surveys Nic's handiwork. "Bondi *in flagrante delicto*."

Bondi groans and starts to wake.

"Quick!" Ty says. "Where's the rag?"

"I've got it." Johnnie refreshes the rag with chloroform. As he rushes back to the bed, Bondi hits out with his arm and Johnnie falls against the side table. The candle topples and amyl flies everywhere. Flames erupt up the side of the bed. Dropping the camera, Nic grabs a pillow and starts to thwack the flames. Yelling that Johnnie's hair is on fire Ty rushes to his aid.

228

I try to hold on to Bondi, but he headbutts me. Rolling off the other side of the bed, he stumbles to the middle of the room. I watch him standing woozily, trying to understand his nakedness. He looks at me, then at the photos lined up along the couch. Realisation dawns. With a sob, he snatches up the photos, grabs at his clothes and runs for the stairs. Scrambling after him, I hear Johnnie sing out nonchalantly, "You forgot the one with a dick in your mouth."

Bondi pivots at the head of the stairs and looks back with desperation. That's when he loses balance. Hands wheel, photos fly, and he plummets. His head, arse, elbows, knees, all thudding like a clatter of hooves. As if Psycho or Pomp were bolting down.

Silence.

Naked, I step over to the railing and peer down upon Bondi's twisted head and limbs. The photos lay about him like confetti. His eyes lock on mine and he lets out a shuddering breath.

I turn to the others, "I think he broke his neck."

Ty joins me at the railing, saying, "Fire's out." He gazes down. "Looks like he's dead."

Nic runs down the stairs and feels for Bondi's pulse. He gazes back up at the three of us.

"Nothing," he says.

"Karma's a bitch," Johnnie says, pressing a wet tea-towel to the burnt side of his head.

Watching Nic gather up the fallen photos, Ty says, "There was no photo with a dick in his mouth."

"Yeah, but he didn't know that."

I pull on my pants. "What do we do now?"

"You and Johnnie stay with the body. Ty will come with me to get the horse and wagon," Nic says.

"Won't Bill Posters get suspicious?" Johnnie says.

"Night collection and internment are a regular occurrence outside curfew," Nic says. "Especially if the fridges are full, or if there's a contamination issue.

We'll just light a contamination flare. That'll scare anyone from investigating too closely."

I follow Ty and Nic down the stairs so I can lock the door after them. One at a time we step over the corpse. "We'll be back as soon as we can," Nic says.

I close and lock the garage door and take my time returning to the body.

Fully clothed, Johnnie comes down to sit on the stairs with me. "Can't we throw something over his face? It's like he's staring at me."

A shuddering intake of breath sends paroxysms of horror up my spine.

"Jesus! He's alive!"

"Nic and Ty said he was dead!"

"They were wrong!"

"What are we going to do?"

"I don't know, but we've got to fix this."

"Why can't we just put him in the coffin when it gets here," Johnnie says. "And close the lid?"

"Bury him alive? Nic won't be into that."

"Well, let's just wait for them to come back."

"We can't leave everything for Nic and Ty," I say. "They do all the hard jobs. We need to step up."

"What do you mean?"

"We should kill him."

A tear rolls down Bondi's cheek.

"I almost feel sorry for him," Johnnie says.

"You wouldn't if you'd seen what he did to Andy or heard the screams of the poor fellas he chased off the cliffs."

"How should we do it?" Johnnie says quietly.

"Have you got a plastic bag?"

"Only cling film for my sandwiches when I used to chauffeur."

"That'll do."

Bondi's eyes beg mine as Johnnie climbs up the stairs and heads for the kitchenette.

"Don't," he manages to gasp.

"What would you have us do?" I say. "Take you to hospital? Drop you at the wall? That'd be our death warrant. And anyway, you've done this to yourself. How long did you think you'd get away with it?"

His mouth moves but no words come out.

"I remember your goading, showing-off for your girlfriend the moments before you pulled the trigger and murdered our friend," I say.

Bondi's eyes blink furiously.

Johnnie returns with the cling wrap and hands it to me.

"Let's get this over with before Nic and Ty get back," I say.

"What do you want me to do?"

"Lift his head."

"His head's heavy," Johnnie says. "Do you think he's in any pain?"

"I don't care," I say, and focus on working with the plastic wrap, which is a nightmare. I wait for some sort of emotion to hit but feel nothing. "Damn I hate this stuff. Why won't it stick? And when it does stick it's only to itself!"

"You've got no patience," Johnnie says as if the only thing that matters is to do a mundane task well. "Take the roll out of its container and wrap it round like it's masking tape. Watch that serration, it's sharp."

I want to work quickly but I'm slow and messy like a kid wrapping a Christmas present.

Bondi's chest heaves, and tremors run through his shoulders and hips. His eyes are just visible through the layers of wrap like someone frozen beneath ice.

"There, done," Johnnie says. "Now stop looking at him."

"How long do you think?"

"Two to three minutes max," Johnnie says. "I'll time it by his wristwatch."

Johnnie lifts up Bondi's twisted arm and gazes into the glass face. Bondi's chest shudders.

"Thank God, he's paralysed." Johnnie says, "or else he'd be flopping all over the place."

"He just shit himself."

Johnnie drops the arm and gets up to climb the stairs.

231

"Don't leave me here alone!" I say.

"I'm just getting some things to mop up his mess."

I hear Johnnie moving about in the loft when a cloud of moths descends and coalesces into a physical shape. The Grim Reaper. I've never been this close. The picture of him as a human-like figure is wrong. The Grim Reaper is a giant insect. The hooded cloak is folded wings and its scythe is a long sucker that attaches to Bondi's forehead. I watch Bondi's soul get suctioned up the translucent pipe, pass through the upper thorax, and drop into the creature's abdomen. The Grim Reaper is a soul processing machine. The insect shudders and ejects Bondi out its anus. Bondi's ghost flumps down the remaining stairs and rolls like a maggot across the floor. He can't elevate like the other ghosts, not even a foot off the ground. He will never fly anywhere. He wriggles through the garage wall and disappears. The Grim Reaper breaks into a thousand moths and flutters into shadow.

Johnnie returns with a bucket of hot soapy water and a sponge. "Thank Christ for the smell of eucalyptus, hey?"

"I just saw the Grim Reaper suck out Bondi's soul."

"I'm surprised he had one."

We leave Bondi's head covered in plastic till we hear the clip-clopping of Psycho and Pomp getting closer.

We strip off the plastic and dump it in the shit bucket.

"Our little secret, okay?" I say to Johnnie. "We don't want Nic to feel bad that he made a mistake. He's under a lot of stress."

"Our secret forever." Johnnie picks up the bucket and heads for the toilet.

I hold the door open for Nic and Ty to carry in the plain wooden coffin. It's a relief to see them.

"Any trouble?" Nic says.

"None."

"Where's Johnnie?" Ty says.

"In the loo," I say.

Together we lift the body and place it in a coffin. We neither cover it nor say any prayer. Before we close the lid Nic tosses in the photographs. He pulls off Bondi's signet ring and slides the watch over his hand.

"What do you want with those?" I say.

"You'll see."

"Shouldn't we keep the photos just in case?" Ty says.

"It's over," Nic says. "We don't need reminders."

We light the carriage torches and load the coffin in feet first. Dressed in our burial garb we begin the slow walk to the cemetery. I ring the bell. Instead of *So Long. So Long. So Long,* I ring: *Stay Gone. Stay Gone. Stay Gone.*

There's always a hole waiting. Nic learnt a long time ago to be prepared. We lower the box and heap dirt over it. The green Boundary Rider – Crème de Menthe – rolls past. It doesn't stop. It's a good omen. Our breath is fresh.

*

The next time the Countess comes in disguised as a wall technician, Nic hands her the package containing Bondi's watch, and signet ring, with instructions to post it from somewhere on the north coast. The package also contains Bondi's suicide note which Nic took ages to write copying the handwriting from the address book Bondi had carried in his pocket.

Hey Little Brother,

Here is Grandfather's signet ring and my watch. I cannot live like this anymore. I let you down. I am a faggot. I always known it. That's why I hounded them off the cliffs. That's why I hate them. I have the infection and cannot end up in GRID. I have swum out to sea to give my foul body to the man eaters.

Forget me. I am nothing.

.21.

"No! Nobody sleeps in me mother's bedroom," Cyril growls when pressed on the matter.

"It's a shrine to her isn't it, Cyril?" Nic says.

"Too bloody right!"

Cyril's two-bedroom terrace is the only house in the Grid that's remained billet free. He threatened the Emergency Response Committee with violence when they came knocking seeking rooms for new internees.

Nic advocated on his behalf and explained Cyril was a war veteran suffering paranoia and should be left alone. He promised to keep an eye on him. The ERC backed off.

"Why does Nic care so much about Cyril?" I ask Ty.

"Cyril helps fill the void left by his dad's passing."

Cyril isn't just a symbolic father, he's also a keeper of secrets, and Nic, just like a son, doesn't tell him everything.

"Where'd you get these?" Cyril says, as Nic hands over Bondi's gun and overalls, saying, "Add these to your stash."

"You don't want to know."

"If that's the answer then I won't argue."

Cyril takes the items and disappears down the corridor.

"What else has he got hidden back there?" Johnnie asks.

"I'm not sure of the full extent but I know there's a grenade," Nic says.

Johnnie shakes his head. "He told me, that first night the wall went up, he's kept things from the war that'd cause the Hygiene Army grief."

"He's got a lot of souvenirs," I say, gazing into the glass hutch full of badges, medals, and other bits of military and personal paraphernalia.

The others come and peer through the glass at the different objects.

Johnnie points at a framed photo of a boy on a bike, "From the looks of things he's lived in this house his whole life."

Cyril, returning, hears Johnnie's words. "I did laddie, except when at war. Right up till me ma died nine years ago, God rest her soul."

"I'm sorry for your loss," Johnnie murmurs.

Cyril nods. "Best woman that ever lived." His eyes well up. "Tended me wounds – mental as well as physical. All she wanted was some grandkids and I failed her."

"You never married, Cyril?" Johnnie says.

"None would have me. I was a wreck." He turns abruptly towards the back of the house. "Come into the kitchen where there's more light. I can't offer you anything except water."

"Nothing wrong with H2O," Nic says as we head down the short corridor to the kitchen.

"Ha!" Cyril says, glad for the subject change. "Except if you're up to your neck in it. Me first job when I was twelve-years-old was cleaning that old factory down on Printers Lane."

"Here we go," Nic pretends exasperation.

"Get stuffed!" Cyril laughs. "Anyway, as I was saying, I found a trapdoor in the floor that lead to an underground creek. Being a dumb, curious, lad, I had to investigate. It started raining, didn't it. Poured down. Water rose quick. Discovered the way was too small for a human to navigate! It was an adventure until I was up to my neck in it. Had to cling to the tunnel roof for my life. Almost drowned. Lost me mum's torch. Found it washed up under the Woolloomooloo wharf after I managed to crawl back out the way I got in."

Nic is confused.

"Are you talking about Busby's Bore?"

"No, ya twit," Cyril scolds. "Busby's another thing entirely."

"What's Busby's Bore?" Johnnie says.

"Busby's Bore's is a convict built, water tunnel that runs from the old swamp where Centennial Park is now," Cyril says, "down under Oxford Street all the way to Hyde Park corner."

235

"Darlinghurst sounds as secure as Swiss cheese," Ty says. "Plenty of ways in and out."

"Busby Bore was filled in with sand when they upgraded the street, but the creek still drains out into Woolloomooloo Bay," Cyril says. "A human can't get through, but other things can."

.22.

The Innocents can't contain Ivy to the Lazaret. She always finds a way into the Grid. She's a climber and a runner. As she hot foots it down the street her laughter bubbles up like fizzy drink. Ghosts swarm to her effervescence and elevate on the bubbles. The more she laughs the more the street is emptied. She is our new Opera Lady.

But there's one ghost that can't elevate to climb aboard. It flumps after her but is always left behind.

.23.

At the soup kitchen the soup is now little more than water with a few specks of onion and potato. Food and medicine transports have ceased as the authorities try to starve out information. REWARD notices glued to all Oxford Street light poles promise three course meals and specialist, individualised, medical care. Despite the hunger and the dire health prospects of the internees no one takes the posters seriously.

When Bondi's face flashes up on the soup kitchen's televisions as a 'missing person' we're careful not to display emotion. Joyful whoops erupt from the tables about us. We needn't have worried.

Onscreen, a ubiquitous Bill Posters sits at an office desk leafing through Bondi's personnel file. "He's an exemplary soldier," the man says. "Zealous and brave. The Hygiene Party could do with a lot more like him."

Ossie Austin leans forward with his microphone, "Do you think he was captured in the Grid?"

"The Boundary Riders saw nothing, and our raids found nothing."

"There are rumours he may have been kidnapped by one of the resistance groups operating on the outside," Ossie says. "What's your opinion on that?"

"I don't respond to rumours," the man closes the folder.

"It doesn't look like Bill has any leads," Nic says casually.

The camera films Ossie walking along the South Bondi cliffs. Beside him is Bondi's girlfriend in her orange Hygiene Party uniform. The wind is whipping her face as she stares out to sea. "He loved it here. It was his favourite place," she says, tears streaming down her face. "Whoever has him please let him go. We want to start a family."

"Dodged a bullet there, sweetheart," Ty mutters into his bowl.

A few days later, all mention of the missing Hygiene soldier disappears from the news channels and the search raids stop.

"The suicide letter must have arrived," Nic says. His smile seems larger because of his extreme weight loss. He bursts into a coughing fit that triggers Johnnie then Ty. I'm surrounded by coughing. With the sound comes perspective. The gold didn't work.

Lying alone in my car wreck bed I retrieve the bottle of cufflinks. Don't be too literal, I think, turning it in my hands. The contents shift and drop. What is this ghost laden place? I ask, unscrewing the lid. What does the Grid mean? I reach in and pull out the first link I touch.

I acknowledge the original custodians of the lands where this story is set. Sovereignty was never ceded.

With love and thanks: Dael Allison, Ed Wright, David Musgrave, Karen Wells, Michael Sala, Meg Vertigan, Rosalind Smith, Keri Glastonbury, Patricia Pender, Jo Canham, and Patricia Sheahan. Most of all I thank Helen Garner for her generous friendship and guidance. Finally, I thank Creative Australia/Australia Council for the funding that made this project possible. The Burdekin Hotel Ladies Parlour image is courtesy of the Australian National University Archives.

Printed in Australia
Ingram Content Group Australia Pty Ltd
AUHW020825280224
391049AU00001B/1

9 781923 099067